Freya bit her lip.

She might have got this all wrong. Perhaps she wasn't even pregnant at all? A false positive? A molar pregnancy? Then everyone could go back to their normal lives. Jamie could leave and go on to another post, or back to his country, and she could remain unchanged on the night shift, reveling in the joy of other people's babies and just imagining what it might feel like to hold her own baby...

The technician was smiling. "Everything looks wonderful here."

Freya let out a breath she hadn't realized she'd been holding. "Really?"

"Any history of multiples in either family?"

What?

The technician turned the screen so that Freya and Jamie could see. There, in black and white, was her womb. Filled with not one but *two* babies separated by a very fine line, which meant...

"Twins? Nonidentical twins?"

Dear Reader,

Many years ago, I suffered from panic attacks and anxiety. So much so, I was housebound for a long, long time. No one seemed to understand the fear I had in my heart for such a scary world. Going outside terrified me.

I'd always wanted to write a heroine who had anxiety. Who hid from the world. Getting by as best as she could in such a limited way. But, of course, my heroine was going to get her freedom from her fear, and achieve the happy-ever-after that everyone with anxiety or panic attacks hopes for.

Strength comes from within, but it also helps if you have someone who is prepared to stand by your side and love you no matter what. So I gave Freya the lovely Jamie.

I do hope you enjoy their story!

Louisa xxx

PREGNANT WITH HIS ROYAL TWINS

LOUISA HEATON

Recycling programs
for this product may
not exist in your area.

ISBN-13: 978-1-335-66322-1

Pregnant with His Royal Twins

First North American Publication 2017

Copyright © 2017 by Louisa Heaton

www.Harlequin.com

Printed in U.S.A.

Books by Louisa Heaton

Harlequin Medical Romance

Visit the Author Profile page at Harlequin.com.

This book is for anyone who suffers from anxiety.
Who has to find the courage from deep within
just to leave the house. It's an endless battle,
but this book is for you.

xxx

CHAPTER ONE

FREYA SURREPTITIOUSLY SLIPPED the packet from her locker and into her uniform pocket, hiding it under her notepad. The lack of her period and the increasing nausea she was experiencing each morning seemed obvious signs enough, but Freya wanted proof. Scientific proof.

Night shift it might be, but to her this was morning, and walking into the staff room and smelling the strong coffee that had been put on to brew had almost made her share with everyone the ginger biscuits she had forced down for breakfast. It had taken a gargantuan effort to control her stomach, and a sheen of sweat had prickled her brow and top lip as she'd fumbled with her locker. Her fingers had almost tripped over themselves in her haste.

Heading to the ladies' loo, she told Mona she'd just be five minutes and that she'd catch up to her at the staff briefing in a moment.

'Okay, hun, see you in five.' Mona smiled and

headed off, her hand clutched around a mug of that nausea-inducing coffee.

The toilets were right next door to the hub, so Freya slipped in and locked the door behind her, leaning back against it, letting out a long, slow breath of relief. She took a moment to stand there and see if her stomach settled.

There didn't seem any doubt about what was happening to her, but she needed to do this just the same. She pulled the pregnancy test from her pocket and stared hard at it, not quite believing that she was actually going to.

She'd always *hoped* that one day she would become a mother. But the actual chances of that ever happening to her had—she believed—become very slim the day she had been scarred for life. Because who would want her now?

'Come on, Freya...you're better than this,' she whispered to herself, trying to drum up the courage to get herself through the next few minutes.

Freya loved the nightshift, working on Maternity here at Queen's Hospital. There was something extra-special about working nights. The quiet. The solitude. The intimate joy of bringing a new life into the world and being with that family as they watched their first sunrise together. A new day. A new family. Life changing. Getting *better*. New hopes. New dreams. There weren't the distractions of daytime—telephones constantly ringing, visiting families all over the place. It was secluded. Fewer busybodies.

It was the perfect hiding place for her, the hospital at night time, and those nights afforded Freya the anonymity that she craved. Lights were kept low. There were shadows to stay in, no harsh fluorescent lighting to reveal to her patients the true extent of her scarring.

It was better now than it had been. She had some smooth skin now, over her cheeks and forehead, where just two years before she'd had angry red pits and lines, her face constantly set and immovable, like a horrific Halloween mask.

Not now. Not now she'd had her many, *many* reconstructive surgeries. Thirty-three times under the skilled scalpel of her plastic surgeon.

And yet she was still hiding—even more so— in a bathroom. Her hands sweating and fidgety as she kept glancing down at the testing kit.

'Only one thing to do, really,' she told herself aloud, shaking her head at the absolute silliness of giving herself a pep talk.

She peed on the stick and laid it on the back of the sink as she washed her hands and then took a step back. She stared at her reflection in the mirror, refusing to look down and see the result. She saw the fear in her eyes, but she also recognised something she hadn't seen for years—*hope*.

'This is what you've always wanted,' she whispered.

But wanting something and actually *achieving* it, when you believed it to be impossible, was another thing altogether. If it *were* possible then she'd finally get her childhood dream. To hold her own child in her arms and not just other people's. To have her own baby and be a mum. Even if that meant she'd have to revert back to living in sunlight. With all those other people.

Even if they didn't stare at her, or do that second glance thing, she still felt that they were looking. It was human nature to look at someone different and pretend that you weren't. And your face was the hardest thing to hide.

Still...this wasn't exactly how she'd imagined it happening. As a little girl she'd dreamt of marrying a handsome man, having his babies and being in a settled relationship.

She had no one. Even 'the guy' had been a mad, terrific impulse, when her body had been thrumming with joy about the fact that she was out amongst people, having fun, enjoying a party behind the veil of her fancy dress costume.

It had been so long since she'd last been to a social event. Too long. Years since she'd stood in a room full of people, chatting, laughing at poor jokes, being *normal*.

Mike had taken that away from her. That joy

and freedom. His jealous actions had imprisoned her in a world of night and pain, surgeries and hiding. Feeling unable to show her face to the world without fearing people's reactions. A frightened child turning away as if to clutch her mother's skirts when a stranger did a double-take and tried not to look appalled or disgusted or worse.

The veil she'd worn that night had hidden everything. The high-necked Victorian steam punk outfit had hidden the scars on her neck that had not yet been tackled, and the veil had added a note of mystery.

That night people had looked at her with intrigue and with delight. They'd smiled…they'd complimented her on how *wonderful* she looked. Their words had made her giddy with happiness. She'd been normal there. Like them.

And then *he'd* been there. The guy. The pirate. He'd seemed uncomfortable. Had appeared to be waiting for enough time to pass so he could make his escape.

She knew how that felt. She'd felt a kind of companionship with him, despite their not having exchanged a word.

It had helped, of course, that he had seductively dark eyes and a wickedly tempting mouth, and she'd almost stopped herself. She'd taken a moment to register the fact that she was *attracted*

to a man when the very idea of that had been
anathema to her for so many years.

But not that night. The costume, the veil, had
given her a sense of bravery she hadn't felt for
a long time.

'I'm Freya. Pleased to meet you.'

'Jamie.'

*'I saw you eyeing up the exit. Getting ready
to make a break for it?'*

'I've been thinking about it.'

*'Please don't. Stay for a little while longer. Let
me get you a drink.'*

It had been crazy how emboldened she'd
felt. Her entire body had been thrumming with
adrenaline and serotonin, her heart pounding
like a revved-up engine. She'd felt alive, happy,
normal again—having a conversation with an attractive man, feeling the thrill of first attraction.

Silly. Childish, maybe, when she really ought
to have known better, but it had just felt so good!

He had made her feel that way. The way he'd
looked at her, his eyes sparkling with inky delight, his full lips curved in a wicked smile. He'd
laughed with joy at her anecdotes, had genuinely
seemed happy to stay.

She'd felt warm and wanted again. Desire had
filled her the second he'd let go of the stem of his
glass and let his fingers trail delicately over the
back of her hand. She'd focused on that move-

ment, watched his fingertips on her skin—her very sensitive skin. She'd looked up and met his eyes, and the most extraordinary question had left her lips.

'Are you married?'

'No.'

'With someone?'

'No.'

'Do you want to be?'

She'd startled herself with the sheer audacity of her question. That wasn't *her*! Freya MacFadden did not proposition strange men!

She'd pulled her hand away then, retreating into the shell she was so accustomed to being inside. But then he'd reached for her hand again. Not to stop her from running away. Not to try and possess her or control her. But just to get her to make eye contact with him.

'I'm guessing you didn't mean to say that?'

'No.'

'Then we can both forget it. Don't worry.'

'I'm sorry.'

'Don't ever be.'

He'd been so kind. So understanding. So she hadn't bolted and neither had he.

They'd continued to sit with each other and talk about what the other guests were wearing and why the charity they were there to support was so important. They'd laughed and had a good time, enjoying each other's company.

He'd offered to walk her out at the end, and she'd let him, intending to say goodbye at the door. To fetch her coat and leave. For ever to remain an enigmatic stranger at a party that he would remember with fondness. Like Cinderella leaving the ball at midnight, only without the glass slipper.

Freya let out a deep breath. She couldn't stay here in the bathroom for too long. There was a hand-over from the day shift.

Freya loved her daytime colleagues, and they her, but she was happy when they went home. Because then she could begin to craft the intimacy that the night shift brought. Lowering the lights. Softening the voices.

It was time.

She couldn't wait any longer.

It was now or never.

She looked down.

And sucked in a breath.

'I'm pregnant.'

She looked back at her reflection, disbelieving. 'I'm *pregnant*?'

She didn't know whether to laugh hysterically or to cry, to gasp or anything else!

She was pregnant.

There was no question as to *how* it had happened. She remembered that night all too well. The father of her child was quite clear in her mind. How could he *not* be? Even if she didn't actually know *who* he was. Or where he came from.

Their meeting that night had been quite by chance—as sudden and exciting and as passionate as she'd imagined it could be. Scary and exhilarating, and one of the best nights of her life. She'd thrown caution to the wind and felt fully alive again for just a moment. For one desperate moment she had been someone else.

She had gone to the ball knowing she would be able to hide behind her veil and costume all night. It had been very gothic-looking, high-necked, with lots of black and dark purple, layers and petticoats. And there had been a top hat, embellished with a large swathe of plum ribbon, copper cogs and whatnots, and a veil of amethyst silk covering her nose and mouth like a Bedouin bride, leaving only her eyes visible.

Her best feature. The only part of her face not scarred or damaged by the acid. She'd been lucky in that respect. Most acid attack victims were blinded.

Her dashing admirer had tried to remove her veil when he'd leant in to kiss her, but she'd stopped him.

'Don't, please. It's better this way.'

He'd smiled and used his mouth in other ways…

Now everyone at the hand-over would be waiting for her, and they'd all look at her when she went back through. The longer she left it, the worse it would be.

She put the cap on the test stick and slipped it into her pocket, then unlocked the bathroom door. Shoulders back, trying to feel relaxed, she headed off to the briefing.

Okay. I can do this. I'm an expert at pretending everything is fine.

The staff were all gathered around the hub of the unit. Whenever a new patient was admitted, or whenever family came to visit, they would walk down this one corridor that led to the hub. From there they would be directed down different corridors—to the right for postnatal and discharges, straight ahead for medical assessment and long-stay patients, to the left for labour and delivery, and beyond that, Theatre.

From the hub, they could see who was trying to buzz through the main doors to gain access to the ward, with the help of a security camera. They could also see the admissions boards, listing who was in which bed and what stage they were at.

There were usually thank-you cards there, perched on the desk, or stuck to the wall behind them, along with a tin or a box of chocolates kindly donated by a grateful family, and on the walls were some very beautiful black and white photographs of babies, taken by their very skilled photographer Addison.

Senior midwife Jules was leaning up against the hub, and she smiled when she saw Freya coming. 'Here she is! Last but not least.'

Freya sidled in amongst the group, keeping her eyes down and trying desperately to blend in. She could feel all eyes upon her and folded herself down into a chair to make herself smaller. She had kept people waiting when they just wanted to go home.

She gratefully accepted a copy of the admissions sheet that Mona passed over to her.

'It's been a busy day today, and it looks like you girls aren't going to have it easy tonight either. In the labour suite, we've got two labouring mums. In Bed One is Andrea Simpson—she's a gravida one, para zero at term plus two days, currently at three centimetres dilated and comfortable, but she had a spontaneous rupture of membranes at home. She's currently on the trace machine and will need to come off in about ten minutes. In Bed Two we have Lisa Chambers, she's a gravida three, para four. Two lots of twins and currently about to deliver her first singleton baby. She's had two previous elective Caesareans and is trying for a VBAC on this one.'

Freya nodded, scribbling notes. A VBAC was a vaginal birth after Caesarean—a 'trial of scar', as some people put it, to see if the mother could deliver vaginally.

'She's labouring fast. At six-thirty she was at six centimetres and she's currently making do on gas and air.'

Freya sat and listened to the rest of Jules's assessment. They had in total twenty-one patients: two on the labour ward, seven on Antenatal and twelve on Postnatal, five of whom were post-surgery.

And the phones would continue to ring. There would also be unexpected walk-ins, and no doubt A&E would send up one or two.

But she didn't mind. Her job was her life. Her passion. The only thing that brought her real joy. It was all she'd ever wanted to be, growing up. A midwife and a mum. And, as of ten startling minutes ago, it looked as if she was going to achieve being both of those.

Freya was excellent at her job, and she truly believed she was only so good at it because it was something she adored doing. Every new baby born was a minor miracle. Every witnessed birth a joy and a privilege. Every moment she sat and held a mother's hand through a contraction was another courageous moment.

It was a weird place, Maternity. A place where staff and patients met often for the first time, total strangers, and then just hours later Freya would know so much about a person—about their family, their hopes and dreams, their sense of humour, what their favourite foods were, what they craved, what they wanted to be, what they wanted to name their children...

She saw them at their worst, but more often at their best and bravest, and when her patients left Freya knew she would always be remembered as being a part of that family's life. Someone who had shared in their most special and cherished moments. Never to be forgotten.

It was an immense responsibility.

Jules put down her papers. 'Now, ladies, I want you to calm yourselves, but we have in our midst a new midwife! His name's Jamie and he's hiding at the back. Give us all a wave, Jamie!'

Jamie? No. Relax. It's a common name.

Freya didn't want to turn and look. She knew how that would make the poor guy feel, having all those women turning and staring at him, eyeing him up. But she knew that it would look odd if hers was the only head that didn't turn. It would single her out. So she gave him a quick glance.

Lovely. No...wait a minute...

She whipped her head back round, her mind whirling, and pretended to scribble some more notes about what Jules had just reported on her sheet. But her pen remained still above the paper.

It's him. It's him! Oh, God, oh, God, oh...

Her trembling fingers touched her lips and her nausea returned in a torrent so powerful she thought she might be sick with nerves right there and then—all over Mona's shoes. She wanted to get up and bolt. Run as fast as she could. But it was impossible.

She frantically eyed the spaces between the rows of staff and wondered how quickly she could make a break for it at the end of the briefing.

It couldn't be possible. How *could* it be him? Her one-night stand.

'Jamie is with us for a couple of months, filling in for Sandra who's away on maternity leave, so I'd like to say welcome to the team, Jamie, it's good to have you here. For the rest of you—Jamie has been working all over the country in various midwifery posts, so he's got a lot of experience, and I hope you'll all take the time to welcome him here, to Queen's.'

Jules smiled.

'Right, then. We're all off. Have a good shift, ladies. And Jamie!'

She smiled, waved, and the majority of staff disappeared off to the locker room, to grab their things and go.

Freya, frozen to the spot, wished she could do the same.

Okay, so the simplest thing to do is to stay out of his way.

So far she'd done a sterling job of that.

Mona was showing him around, pointing out where everything was, getting him acquainted with the temperamental computer and how to admit people to the ward—that kind of thing. Freya, on the other hand, had just been given the task to introduce herself to the two labouring mothers and work on the labour ward—which she was very happy about because that gave her the opportunity to stay in her patients' rooms and not see or have to engage with *him*.

The irony of the situation was not lost on her. The first time they had met she had been brimming with temporary confidence, an urge to experience life again as a normal woman meeting a handsome guy at a party. But now she was back to reality. Hiding and skulking around corners, trying her best to avoid him. The man she'd propositioned.

And what the hell were the odds of him turning up on the very same day that she took a pregnancy test? It had to be millions to one, didn't it? Or at the very least a few hundred thousand to one?

Jules had said he'd been working in various posts around the country. Why hadn't he got a job at one of those? Why did he keep moving?

What's wrong with him?

The weight of the pregnancy test in her left pocket seemed to increase, its weight like a millstone.

She entered Andrea Simpson's room quietly.

'Hello, it's Andrea, isn't it? I'm Freya and I'm going to be your midwife tonight.'

She smiled at her new charge and then glanced over at her partner, who was putting his phone in his back pocket and standing up to say hello.

He reached over to shake her hand and she saw him do that thing with his eyes that everyone did when they noticed her face—noticed that she'd been burned, somehow, despite her corrective surgery and skin grafts. Noticed that she'd had *work done.*

His gaze flittered across her features and then there was *that* pause.

'Hi, I'm George,' he introduced himself. 'I'm just here to do what I'm told.'

Freya smiled. 'Mum's the boss in this room.'

She glanced over at the belt placement on Andrea's abdomen and checked the trace on the machine. The trace looked good. No decelerations and the occasional contraction, currently seven or eight minutes apart. Still a way to go for Andrea.

'I want you to stay on this for ten more minutes, then I'll take it off—is that all right?'

Andrea nodded, reaching for a bottle of water and taking a short drink.

'Do you have a birth plan?'

'Just to have as much pain relief as I can get.'

'Okay. And what sort of pain relief are you thinking of?'

'I want to start with gas and air, see how I go with that, and then maybe get pethidine. But I'm open to whatever you suggest at the time.'

Freya smiled. 'So am I. This is *your* birth, *your* body. I'll be guided by you as long as it's safe. Okay?'

'Yes...'

Freya could see that Andrea had questions. 'Nervous?'

Andrea giggled. 'A bit. This is all so *new*!'

Tell me about it.

Freya had seen hundreds of babies come into the world. She never tired of it. Each birth was different and special, and now she knew that if all went well and she didn't miscarry she'd be doing this herself in a few months. Lying on a bed...labouring. It was actually going to happen.

'You'll do fine.'

She laid a reassuring hand on her patient's and wondered who'd be there to hold *her* hand during labour? Her mum?

Her mind treacherously placed Jamie beside her bed and she felt goosebumps shiver down her skin.

No. It can't be him.

It can't be.

But isn't that what you always wanted? A cosy, happy family unit?

It had been. Once.

It was *her*. He'd have known those blue eyes anywhere. The eyes that had been haunting his dreams for weeks now.

He'd been invited to that charity ball after he'd attended a small event in Brighton that was meant to have been low-key. But word must have reached the ears of the hospital that the heir to the throne of Majidar, Prince Jameel Al Bakhari, was around and an invitation had got through to his people.

It had been for such a good cause he hadn't been able to refuse it. A children's burns unit. He'd seen the damage burns could cause, from a simple firework accident right through to injuries sustained in a war zone, and it was shocking for anyone. A painful, arduous road to recovery.

But for it to happen to a child was doubly devastating.

So he'd attended, dressed as a pirate, complete with a large hoop earring and a curved plastic scimitar that had hung from his waist by a sash.

He'd not intended to stay for very long. He'd made them keep his presence there quiet, as he didn't enjoy people bowing and scraping around him. He hated that whole sycophantic thing that happened around members of his royal family. It was part of why he'd left Majidar. To be a normal person.

It was why he tried to live his life following his passion. And his passion was to deliver babies. Something that was not considered 'suitable' for a prince back in his own country.

But what could you do when it was your calling? Delivering babies was what he had always yearned to do, and he'd never been destined for the throne. His elder brother had been the heir and was now ruler. So surely, he'd reasoned, it was better to spend his life doing something worthwhile and selfless instead of parading around crowds of people, smiling and waving, a spare heir that no one needed?

He'd faced some considerable opposition. Mostly from his father, who'd been appalled that his second son wanted to do what he viewed as 'women's work'. His father had forbidden him ever to speak of it again and, respecting his father, he had kept that promise. Until his father had passed away. Then his brother Ilias had taken the throne, and Jamie had approached his new King and told him of his vocation.

Ilias had proudly granted his younger brother the freedom to pursue it.

So he'd gone to the ball, telling the organisers that he didn't want to draw attention to himself, and asking that they did not make any special announcement that he was there, just let him join in as any other person would.

Jamie had mingled, smiled, shaken people's hands—and found himself losing the will to live and wondering when would be a polite time to leave… And then he'd spotted *her* in a corner of the room.

Almost as tall as he, she'd been dressed from top to toe in black, accented in dark purple, with some weird cogs and a strange pair of pilot goggles attached to her hat. Her face had been covered by a Bedouin-style gauze veil that had reminded him of home.

Her honey-blonde hair had tumbled down her back, almost to her waist, and above that veil had sparkled the most gorgeous blue eyes he had ever seen. Blue like the ocean and the sky, and just as wild and free.

'I'm Freya. Pleased to meet you.'

'Jamie.'

'I saw you eyeing up the exit. Getting ready to make a break for it?'

He had been. But not any more.

So he'd stayed. And they'd talked. And laughed.

Freya had been delightful, charming and intelligent, and so easy to be with. She'd told him a story about the last time she'd attempted to flee a party. She'd been eleven years old and it had been the first time her parents hadn't stayed with her. She'd been frightened by all the noise and all the people and had scurried away when no one was looking and run home to hide in her dad's garden shed.

She'd grimaced as she'd recalled how she'd stayed there, terrified out of her wits not only about being found out, but also because there had been a massive spider in the corner, watching her. He'd laughed when she'd told him she'd almost peed her pants because her bladder had been killing her from drinking too much pop. But she hadn't been able to go home too early, or her parents would have known that she'd run away.

'No spiders here,' he'd said.

'No.'

'Nothing to be afraid of. I'll protect you.'

'Now, why would you do that? You hardly know me. I might be dangerous.'

'I think I can handle you.'

His pulse had thrummed against his skin, his temperature rising, his whole body aware. Of *her*. She hadn't removed the veil, but she'd kept on peering at him over it with devilment in her gaze, and he'd felt drawn to her excitement and bravado. She hadn't been drunk on alcohol. Her eyes had been clear, pupils not pinpointed, so no drugs. But she'd definitely been intoxicated by *something*, and he'd begun to suspect that he was feeling the same way, too.

There'd been something about her. So different from everyone else at the party. But what had it been? What had made her unique? Had it been the veil? The air of mystery? Or just those eyes? Eyes that had looked so young, but had also spoken of a wisdom beyond her years. As if she knew something that no one else did. As if she'd experienced life and the gamut of emotions that came with it. And yet that night she'd been drawn to him, and he to her. She a purple and black veiled moth and he the flame.

'Do you trust me?'

She'd smiled. *'Can any woman trust a pirate?'*

'I'm not just a pirate.'

The corners of her mouth had twitched and she'd glanced at his mouth, then back to his eyes, and he'd been hit with such a blow of lust he hadn't been able to help himself. He'd tried to look away, to take a deep breath, to regain control over his senses.

'I need to go,' she'd said.

'Let me walk you home.'

'No need. I have transport.'

'Then let me walk you to it.'

He'd offered her his arm and she'd taken it, smiling through the gauze and looking up at him, her eyes gleaming.

He'd been overcome by a bolt of desire.

But what to do about it? He considered himself a gentleman. He had principles…he'd only just met her…but there was *something*…

They'd stood there staring at each other, each of them trying to force the words to say goodbye, but neither of them ready to leave just yet. Her eyes had glinted at him in the darkness, with a look that said she wanted more than this…

The first door they'd tried had been unlocked, and they'd found themselves inside a supply closet, filled with clean linen and pressed staff uniforms.

He'd stood in front of her, just looking at her, noticing the small flecks of green and gold in her eyes. They'd shone like jewels, and her pupils had been large and black as she'd reached for his shirt and pulled him close.

He'd lost himself in her. Completely forgotten who he was, where he was. All that had mattered had been the feel of her, the taste of her, as he'd hitched up her skirts, her million and one petticoats, slid his hands up those long, slim legs…

Freya…

Like two lost souls that had found each other, they had clutched and grasped, gasped and groaned. He'd reached to remove the veil, so that he could kiss her, so that he could seek out her lips and claim her for his very own, but she'd stopped him, stilled his hand.

'Leave it. Please.'

'But, Freya…'

'No kissing…please.'

He'd respected her wishes. That veil had made her seem like forbidden fruit. An enigma. Her hat had fallen to the floor and her long blonde locks had tumbled around her shoulders like golden waves. And the dark stockings on her ever so creamy thighs had aroused a feeling in him that he'd never quite experienced before.

They'd given each other everything.

And when they were spent they had slumped against each other and just stood there, wrapped in each other. Just breathing. Just existing. It was all that they'd needed.

A sound by the door had made them break apart and rearrange their clothing.

She'd glanced at him, guiltily. *'I must go.'*

He'd stared at her, not knowing what to say.

He'd felt as if there was so much he *wanted* to say to her, but it had all got stuck in his throat and he'd remained silent. He'd wanted to tell her to stay. To come back to the hotel with him. He'd wanted to ask her if he could see her again and that had both shocked and scared him—because he *never* made commitments.

But she'd slipped from the closet, and by the time he'd adjusted his clothes and made himself presentable again she'd been gone.

He'd scanned the ballroom, looking for her fall of blonde hair, looking for those all-seeing eyes, but she'd gone.

Jamie had signalled his security people and told them to look out for her, to check the car park, but like an enigmatic spy she had simply disappeared. Disappointed, he had got into his own car and been driven home.

But now she was here.

She'd turned to look at him after Jules had asked everyone to welcome him. She was *here*. Of all the places in the world he could have looked. In this hospital. On this ward. With him. Those eyes of hers had pierced his soul once again, reawakening his dormant desire and making every cell of his body cry out for her.

But there'd been something else. Something that had rocked him. Something he hadn't noticed before. And now he understood about the veil.

Freya was scarred. Something had happened to her. To her face. She'd had work done. Skin grafts, no doubt. Painful surgeries and recovery. How many? What had happened to her? A house fire? Was that why she'd been at the charity event for the burns unit?

And he'd sensed her fear. Her shock. Had seen the horror in her eyes as she'd realised who he was. Then he'd seen her shame, because she'd noticed how he'd reacted when he saw her properly.

Angry with himself, he'd wanted to reach out, touch her, tell her that she should not be ashamed—but she'd bolted.

Jamie sensed a soul like his own. Someone who preferred the everyday to the limelight. Someone who avoided crowds and adulation. Someone who preferred to hide behind a mask.

He felt her magnetism. Her draw.

And helplessly he allowed himself to be pulled in.

'It is you, isn't it?'

Freya had quickly run to the kitchenette to make her patient's husband a cup of tea. She'd slid into the small room, breathing a sigh of relief, wondering just how the hell she was going to get through work for the next few weeks if *he* was going to be here, covering for Sandra.

She'd just been kneeling down to put the milk back in the fridge when she'd heard the door open behind her and then his voice.

Freya closed her eyes and looked down, hoping the loose tendrils of her hair would cover her face. She didn't want this. Didn't *need* this. Tonight had already been overwhelming—finding out she was pregnant—but to have him here too? To have to have *this* conversation? Now? At work?

'I'm sorry, I need to take this drink to my patient.'

She held the mug of tea in her hand, not turning to face him, but so very aware of his presence behind her in this small, suddenly claustrophobic room.

This man had made her body sing. Nerve-endings that she'd thought were dead had come alive that night and she had felt every single part of her body as he'd played her like a delicate harp. Knowing what to touch and how to touch, how to make her gasp, sigh and groan. She'd experienced things with this man that she had never felt before. He'd made her reveal a side to herself that she'd never known.

But he'd been with a woman who didn't exist

in reality, and she didn't need to see his disappointment when he realised.

Just being this close to him now was doing crazy things to her insides and turning her legs to jelly. And was it hot? Her armpits were tingling with sweat.

They'd had an amazing night. And it would stay that way as long as he didn't ruin the illusion by seeing her for who she really was. He'd probably thought that she was some rare beauty, but if he saw her properly he would soon be surprised. No doubt about that.

She didn't want to have to watch it happen right in front of her. That *look*. She'd already noticed his shock when they were at the hub, and work was meant to be her happy place. He was ruining everything.

Holding the mug of tea before her, she kept her head down to pass him so she could get to the door.

He stepped back, keeping a respectful distance, which she appreciated, but as she reached for the handle he spoke again.

'It *is* you.'

Keeping her eyes downcast, she stared at the floor, not wanting to see him take in her scars, her wounds. To see that she was damaged goods. This man had *wanted* her! Wanted her so badly! And it had been wondrous—a memory she'd cherished since that night. A moment of freedom from the poor existence with which Mike had left her. And she had revelled in that.

Did she want to see him realise that the woman he had given himself to was not the one of his dreams? No. Just for once she wanted to be a good memory for someone. For them to believe her beautiful.

'I'm sorry, I have to go.'

'Look at me.'

'Jamie, please…' She glanced upwards for just a moment and painfully met his gaze, her eyes blurry with unshed tears, waiting to see him realise his mistake…

Only it didn't happen. He simply looked directly at her. Showed no shock this time. No horror.

'If only you knew how much I've wanted to see you again.'

Confused, she stared back. Felt the tears finally escape her eyes and trickle down her cheeks.

'What…?'

What was he saying? What did he mean? Why wasn't he reacting to her face like everyone else did?

'You're unforgettable—do you know that?'

She swallowed hard, looking away, down at the steaming mug. 'For all the wrong reasons.'

She got out of the kitchenette as quickly as she could. What *was* it with them and small rooms? Kitchenettes. Supply cupboards. Was Jamie set to startle her in anything less than six by six? Should she stay away from bathroom cubicles, too?

As she hurried back to her patient's room she madly wiped her eyes and sniffed a few times, to try and look presentable for Andrea and her husband.

What had just happened? How had he managed to turn her understanding of the world completely on its head?

She slipped her hand into her pocket, to reassure herself that the pregnancy test was still there. Only it wasn't. Her pocket was empty except for her notebook and pen.

She looked back to the kitchenette and saw Jamie come out, his face a mass of confused emotions as his eyes met hers.

Over the small white stick in his hand.

CHAPTER TWO

IT MUST HAVE fallen from her pocket. But when? And how?

And then she remembered crouching down to get the milk from the fridge. Something similar had happened before, due to the design of the pocket on her uniform. It was below the waist, low down. She'd lost her mobile phone once that way, hearing it clatter onto the floor. She'd not heard the test stick fall. Probably because she'd heard his voice instead. Felt his presence.

'It is you. Isn't it?'

His words had cut through everything.

Her mind had been on other things. Other concerns. She'd closed that fridge fast. Stood up quickly and made that tea, trying not to look at him, trying to get away as quickly as she could.

She was saved from going over to him and taking the test from his hands. The call light above Bed Two flashed and she went in to see how Lisa Chambers, her labouring mother there, was doing.

Lisa was pacing the room, her abdomen swollen before her, her hands pressed into her back.

'I felt the need to push with that last one, Freya.'

She handed the mug of tea over to Lisa's husband and then guided Lisa back to the bed. 'I'll need to check you before you can push.'

She didn't need Lisa pushing too early. It might cause a swelling of the cervix and make delivery more difficult.

Regaining control of her own body, she checked her patient's. 'You're right, Lisa. You're ten centimetres. You can push with the next contraction.'

Lisa got up off the bed. 'I can't lie down, though.'

'That's fine. Let your body lead you and I'll help. Just tell me when you're ready.'

Lisa beckoned to her husband to stand on the other side of the bed and take her hands. Then she squatted on the other side.

'When the contraction comes, take a big, deep breath, Lisa—chin to your chest and *push*, right into your bottom.'

Lisa nodded, waiting, then closed her eyes and sucked in that breath.

Freya quickly washed her hands, dried them and gloved up. Lisa might be five times a mother, but this was her first vaginal delivery. It might take some time and, with the best will in the world and not wanting to prolong her patient's suffering, she hoped that it would.

Because she herself needed some time before she could leave this room. Needed to think of what she would say. What she would do. How she could escape this situation she'd found herself in.

Lisa was an excellent patient, though, and obviously keen to see her fifth child. Because within forty-five minutes of her first needing to push, her son slithered into Freya's waiting hands.

She passed the baby to his sobbing mother, clamped and cut the cord, then helped Lisa into bed and wrapped a towel around her son to help keep him warm.

The baby cried—bursts of pure sound, a completely new person announcing his arrival. Freya smiled at the newly created family of seven and quietly gave Lisa the injection of syntocinon that would hasten delivery of the placenta, as per her patient's request.

It seemed to take no time at all to deliver it, check it, assess the baby's APGAR score, then Lisa's, and realise that Lisa hadn't torn at all. Her five-pound, twelve-ounce son had arrived perfectly.

There was no reason for Freya to stay at all.

She prided herself on leaving her families to have some private time as soon as she could after the birth. So they could welcome and get to know their new baby on their own. But tonight she hesitated by the door.

'Congratulations, you two.'

'Thanks, Freya. I couldn't have done it without you.'

'Nonsense. You were a model patient.' She smiled, trying to pluck up the courage to go out there and face him. *That* conversation.

She could only hope and pray that he was busy with a patient of his own.

But she had no such luck.

Jamie was just walking back to the hub desk, sliding his pen into his top pocket. His dark eyes instantly met hers. Challenged her. Demanded an explanation.

She almost faltered. But she had Lisa's notes to finish writing up, and when that was done she needed to check on Andrea. She'd taken her off the trace a while ago and she'd been steadily contracting every five minutes the last time she'd seen her.

Jamie stood still as she walked past him, and she hoped he wouldn't see that her nerves were making her hands tremble and shake as she sat down at the desk.

'It's not what you think.' She glanced up at

him, then away again. *Dammit.* He was just as handsome as she remembered. Even more so, this close. He was hauntingly beautiful.

Jamie sat down in the chair next to her. 'What *do* I think?'

She paused, her pen over Lisa's notes. 'It belongs to a patient.'

'A patient?'

'Yes. I must have put it in my pocket without realising and—'

'We don't do pregnancy testing here. Mona was quite clear when she showed me around that the fertility clinic is in a whole other ward next to this one.'

She tried her hardest not to look at him. Not to meet the searing gaze that she knew would instantly divine the truth. If her cheeks could have flamed red, then they would.

She looked at him, guilt filling her eyes.

He gazed at her for a moment, his face deadly serious. 'Tell me the truth. It's yours?'

Her eyes closed, almost as if the admission would cause her pain. 'Yes…' A whisper.

'Am I…?'

The words choked in his throat and she opened her eyes again in anguish. She hardly knew this man. He was a temp. A locum. A drifter. How could she tell this stranger that the baby in her womb was most definitely his? Because she didn't sleep around. She never met anyone—never gave herself the chance to.

She didn't need to get that kind of close to any man, to develop feelings for any man, because look at what had happened to her when she did. She'd suffered more than she'd ever believed it was possible for one body to suffer after getting involved with Mike. The pain she'd gone through, both emotionally and physically, had almost destroyed her.

She never wanted that again. Never wanted to risk it. Having that one night with Jamie—a stranger—had been a moment in which she'd thrown caution to the wind, feeling herself so physically attracted to the pirate she'd met at the ball that she'd decided she would risk it. Keeping her anonymity, she would never have to deal with him afterwards.

Because why *shouldn't* she have slept with him? It was allowed, and it had felt *so good* to let all that other stuff go.

But they'd both been stupid. Believing that one night wouldn't have consequences. Believing that they could walk away.

They should have known the risks.

They'd been wrong! And no one could be angrier with her than she was with herself.

She'd once sat on a hospital bed, with a plastic compression mask over her burnt features, and promised her mother that she would never get involved with another man ever again. Would never cause her family anguish ever again. Because what Mike had done—throwing that acid at her face—hadn't just affected her. The tragedy had affected her family and even Mike's family, who were distraught that their son was in prison.

And all because she'd got involved with him.

And now she was pregnant. With Jamie's baby.

'Yes. You're the father.'

She saw him look down at the ground. Could almost hear the cogs going around in his skull, almost sense his thoughts as he tried to distance himself from her. Maybe even planned to leave this place. Get a temporary post somewhere else less complicated.

'Right.' A pause. 'It's very early on. Four... maybe five weeks?'

She nodded.

'You need to start taking folic acid.'

'I know.'

'You need to look after yourself.'

She knew he was just trying to say the sensible thing, trying to help and maybe trying to make sense of it in his own head. This had to be a huge shock to him too. But to Freya it sounded as if he was telling her what to do, and no man would ever tell her what to do again.

Her control was slipping. 'You don't need to tell me how to do anything. You don't own me.'

'I'm not. I'm just trying—'

'You're just trying to take over! So back off, Jamie, I don't need this in my life!'

She tried her hardest not to shout, but it was difficult. All she wanted to do was run away, but it was as if the walls were closing in and she would soon be trapped with him. A man. A stranger. Tied to him for eternity when she knew nothing about him. He could be anybody.

He sat forward in his chair. 'You're pregnant with *my child*. I don't think you realise what this means.'

She leaned forward too, anger and rage fuelling her bravado, matching his stance. 'I'm a midwife. Of course I know what it means.'

She stood, grabbing her notes and pen, deciding she would check on Andrea. She would finish her notes in there—give Jamie a chance to think about what she'd said.

He was *not* going to tell what to do.

He was going to be a father.

Of course if nothing went wrong they would have to marry. If the people of Majidar ever found out that he'd got a woman pregnant and then abandoned her to have the child alone they'd be appalled. And so would he. He wasn't just a prince, he was a man, and as such he had a responsibility to do the right thing. No child of his would grow up to be illegitimate—he just wouldn't accept it. The baby was his and he would be its father.

Honour in this country was different from honour in his. He saw it on the television every day—men getting women pregnant and then leaving them to raise the child alone. There were single parents everywhere, and that was fine for them—but not for him. Not at all. He could never knowingly sire a child and then abandon it to God only knew what kind of future.

This was *his* child. And, whether Freya liked it or not, he had a duty to it.

And to her.

But what had happened to her? What was making her so frightened and on edge? Why couldn't she look him directly in the eye? Was it her scars? Her face? Did her shame stem from that? Or was it the unexpected pregnancy?

Clearly she was in shock. All he'd tried to do was make this easier for her. Try and shoulder some of the responsibility.

Because it was his and his alone. And because of who he was it was imperative that he do the right thing.

He would need to speak to his advisor.

* * *

At just after six in the morning Andrea delivered a healthy baby girl.

Freya was reluctant to leave her patient's room and go back out there and face Jamie again, but she knew that she had to.

She could only hope that as there was less than one hour until the end of her shift he might be busy elsewhere and she would be able to get through it without having to see him.

She'd had her fill of pushy men. To be fair, she'd only been with one, but that one—Mike— had been enough for two lifetimes.

It had started innocently enough. Mike had asked her not to go out with her friends from college one evening.

'Why not?'

'I just can't bear to imagine you out on the town like that. I've seen gaggles of girls dressed to impress and off their heads on tequila shots. I know what guys think of girls like that, and I don't want them looking at you like you're a piece of meat.'

She'd thought he was being sweet! That he cared so much about her.

He'd begged her not to go, and to make him feel better she'd cancelled. The next week, when the girls had wanted to go out again, rather than just accept the invitation straight away she'd said she needed to check with Mike first.

Slowly she had stopped having any contact with her friends. Then he'd started making comments about how her family looked down their noses at him and how family meet-ups made him uncomfortable—could they stay home?

Bit by bit he had isolated her, until her entire life had been his to control and manipulate. She'd felt as if she couldn't breathe and she'd tried to break away. He'd found her, begged her to stay, promised he would change.

Only he hadn't. If anything he had got worse—his insecurities, his paranoia.

She'd bolted one day when he was at work and run home to live with her mum again. She'd thought she was free, that her life was hers again, until that terrible day on the high street...

Freya was grateful to see that the hub looked clear and she headed over, her back aching slightly, and slumped into a chair to complete Andrea's notes. The open tin of chocolates called her name and she unwrapped one and popped a caramel barrel into her mouth.

Mmm...just what I need.

The chocolate began to soften in her mouth, and as she chewed she realised just how hungry she was. She'd not really taken a proper break whilst Andrea laboured, and suddenly she was starving—craving a full English breakfast, washed down with a mug of strong tea.

A banana was placed right in front of her. She frowned and looked up to see who had given it to her.

'Jamie…'

'Eat this. You haven't had anything all night.'

She moved the banana away from her. 'Thank you, but I have other plans.'

'So you say—but you're not the only one who gets to make decisions about yourself any more. This is my baby too and you need to eat. *Healthily*, preferably.'

He grabbed hold of the tin of sweets and moved it away from her.

Angrily, Freya grabbed the tin back. 'Keep your voice down. I don't need the whole ward hearing about it.'

'Are you going to eat the banana?'

She glanced at the fruit, lying harmlessly on the desk, and felt repulsed by it. The idea of taking a bite of it turned her stomach. She craved hot food. Preferably dripping in grease.

'Not right now.' She felt a little hypocritical. She'd often lectured pregnant women about eating well for a healthy pregnancy and here she was craving fat. And maybe another chocolate from that tin.

'So when are you going to eat?'

'When I get out of here. At home, where I can cook myself something.'

She didn't want to tell him that she didn't like to go out during the day. Didn't like to sit by herself in cafés filled with staring people.

'Where do you live?'

She looked at him incredulously. 'Why would I tell you that?'

'Because, like it or not, we're involved now and I want to look after you.'

'I don't know you!'

'You knew me enough to make a child with me.'

He stared hard at her, his eyes dark and dangerous, as if daring her to try and wriggle out of that one.

'Well, I didn't know I was doing that at the time.'

It was enough to make her remember their assignation—her back against the wall as he hoisted her legs around his waist and thrust into her, her hands frantically grasping at him. Both of them made courageous by darkness and anonymity.

No. She would not tell him her address. He might be anyone and her home was her safe space. Her haven. A place where she could relax and just *be*. It was her bolthole, and there was no way she was going to give him that information.

'You're not going to do this, you know.'

'Do what?'

'Go all alpha on me. Order me about.' She could hear her own voice quaking as she stood up for herself.

'I care about you.'

'No, you don't. You got me pregnant and now you think that you've got to be seen to be doing the right thing. Well, I'm giving you an out. You're off the hook—you can walk away.'

It would be easier, wouldn't it? To do it alone? Without a man? Because men were frightening. They didn't know what it felt like to be a woman. To know that half the population was bigger and physically stronger than you. That they could overpower you if they cared to try. Not to be able to walk down a street without fearing the footsteps you could hear behind you. Always having to be aware of your surroundings. Of who might be looking at you strangely. Were they just curious, or were they about to pounce?

He leaned forward and stared at her. 'I don't know what experiences previous men have given you, but let me tell you something. *I am not that kind of man.* When I do something I take full responsibility for it. And that means taking care of you and taking care of that baby.'

'But you don't have to. I can do it alone.'

'I do have to. It's my child. It has to be honourable.'

'Why does it have to be *honourable*?'

Even as she said the words she realised how childish she sounded. Why wouldn't she want her baby to be honourable? Was she cheapening it already? By saying it didn't matter if it was 'honourable'?

But this was *her* baby! She had dreamt of this for years!

He recoiled as if she'd slapped him, as if he was appalled that she could think anything else.

'Because it has to be. I won't have it any other way.'

She moved the banana. She could smell it and it was beginning to turn her stomach.

'If everything you do is "honourable", then how come you had a quickie with a stranger in a closet? Surely being *honourable* would make you at least a hotel-room-with-satin-sheets kind of man?'

'Maybe I am?' he challenged, pushing the banana back towards her. 'There is plenty that you don't know about me, Freya MacFadden.'

The use of her name made her narrow her eyes as she looked at him. God, he was beautiful. Almond-shaped eyes, dark as ink, cheekbones a model would die for, and his lips...

Oh, goodness, I remember those...

Freya cleared her throat and tried to sound as if she was in control of this conversation. 'Well, perhaps you'd care to enlighten me?'

Jamie checked around them, as if keen to make sure they were alone and no one was listening in.

'I can't tell you right now. You wouldn't believe me. Perhaps if you agreed to meet me here?'

He pulled a card from his uniform pocket and slid it across to her. It was a glossy black card with the name of a hotel in silver.

Why did he want to meet her in a hotel? What kind of movie did Jamie think he was living in? He was deluded. This was normal life. People didn't do that. There was no way she was going to meet a total stranger in a *hotel*!

'Can't you just tell me?'

'You wouldn't believe it. Please meet me there.'

It would be a public place. Safe. But it would be in daylight. When there were other people about. Not in his room. Nowhere they could be alone. But she would have to face other people's stares.

'When?'

'Tomorrow? Before your shift? We do need to talk about this and we can't do it here.'

She could maybe put on some sunglasses and wrap a thick scarf around her neck, then no one would stare at her. She could get there before everyone else was up and milling around for breakfast. She could listen to what he had to say, give him his five minutes, then slink out quietly.

'Fine. About six? That gives us an hour before work.'

'Thank you.'

She nodded, then picked up the banana, gave it back to him and said, 'Now, take that away, please, before I throw up all over this desk.'

His mouth curled slightly at the corners. 'Tomorrow I'll bring you grapes.'

The Franklin Hotel sat atop a hill, so that as Freya drove towards it she had a sense of awe and magnificence as she approached the beautiful Georgian manor. Looking at it from a distance, she wondered how Jamie could afford to stay in such an opulent place.

I don't have to go in. I don't have to hear what he has to say.

But she knew she would. Because, no matter how terrified she felt, she knew that she owed her baby the chance to know something about its father. So she could look her child in the eye and tell him, or her, that she'd tried everything.

It looked welcoming and warm, with yellow lights gleaming out in the darkness of the early morning, the sky above a blue which was fading from inky navy to palest azure.

Parking her little hatchback next to rows of expensive cars with chauffeurs sitting in them made her feel a little uneasy. Why had Jamie asked her to meet him here? What was it that she was about to learn from him?

He was a midwife. A damned sexy one, if she was honest, with an accent to die for and eyes that looked right into her soul and grasped her by the heart. She'd never met anyone like him. The mystery was what could he tell her here that she would never have believed if he'd just told her at work?

Whether she liked it or not, whilst this baby nestled in her womb they would be tied to one another—and Jamie seemed determined to be in her life.

Adjusting her scarf and lowering her sunglasses, she strolled across the gravel driveway, her nerves jittery, her legs weak. In the hotel, gentle music playing from a piano met her ears. To her right was a reception desk, where exquisite and perfectly presented staff waited to attend to every guest's needs.

'May I help you, madam?' asked a young man in a navy suit with enough gel in his hair to sink a ship.

No, it's fine. I'm just leaving.

'I'm supposed to be meeting a Mr Jamie Baker?'

'Miss MacFadden? We've been expecting you.' He smiled, revealing perfectly white teeth. 'Please take the lift to my right and go up to the third floor.'

Take the lift? Go to the third floor? That wasn't meeting in a public space. That meant going to his room. Where there was a bed.

'Oh...um... What room number?'

'Mr Baker has the entire third floor.'

Freya blinked. What? Who went to a hotel and took up an entire floor? That was the sort of thing celebrities did with their entourages, or royalty, or...

You wouldn't believe me if I told you.

What was going on? It was all so confusing. He was just a guy, right? A normal guy.

Was he rich?

The night they'd met at the gala she'd known there was a member of royalty there. She'd heard the rumour but she'd never been introduced to anyone. There'd been no announcement. Everyone had hidden behind their masks and it had been exciting. You could talk to *anyone* and not know it!

Including royalty.

Have sex in a closet with them, if you so chose...

Freya swallowed hard, trying to control her rapidly weakening legs as she hesitantly went over to the lifts and pressed the button.

I could still go. I could run. Just get the hell out of here!

She stood there, fidgeting with the tassels on her scarf, as she waited for the lift to come down to the ground floor.

I owe it to our baby.

Was Jamie a member of some royal family? How could that be?

She thought about turning tail and running—changing her mind and hiding somewhere. Her parents' beach house on Hayling Island, perhaps. It was the place she went when she needed to hide and think. She'd gone there when she'd first been released from hospital, months after the acid attack, and she'd had to wear that damned orthotic burns mask every day, marking her out as different.

She'd felt like a leper. As if there was a bright neon arrow over her head screaming that here was someone *not normal*.

The house on Hayling Island would soon be filling up with summer rentals, but hopefully no one was there right now. Jamie wouldn't know where to find her. It would be good for her to take a break while the morning sickness was in full swing.

The lift pinged, signalling its arrival, and the doors slid open. On the back wall of the lift was an ornate mirror and she gazed at her reflection, wondering what the woman in the mirror should do. Run like hell? It was like staring into a prison.

All ye who enter here...

But Freya had seen more than enough women arrive on her ward to give birth alone, without a father involved, and she had felt sorry for all those children who would grow up without an interested father.

Jamie *wanted* to be involved. He'd said he would not shirk his responsibility. All she'd ever wanted was to be loved and to have a baby—something she'd thought would never happen after her acid attack—and here she was, pregnant and with a guy who said he wanted to be involved. She owed him a chance, the opportunity to show her what he could provide for their child.

With hesitation Freya stepped into the lift and pressed the button for the third floor, eyeing the reception area with longing as the lift doors closed her in.

As the lift ascended she gripped the strap of her bag as if it was a lifeline. An anchor to real life. The sensation that her world was about to change for ever was drowning her in anticipation, and she wished she'd eaten more of those ginger biscuits before coming, because her stomach felt as if it was about to explode.

The lift stopped rising. *Ping!* The doors slid open to reveal two men in dark suits.

Her stomach flipped and she looked from one to the other.

Guards? Why does Jamie need guards?

They were wearing those earpieces that secret service men had on television. They asked her to put her bag through a scanner, and then she had to walk through a metal detector shaped like a doorway before they escorted her down the corridor towards a pair of ornate doors.

What on earth have I got myself into?

Silently she followed, feeling like a little girl between giants. Were they wearing guns beneath their jackets? Her mouth went dry at the thought of it and she gripped her bag tighter, as if that small item would somehow protect her from what was to come.

At ornate double doors the men stopped and grabbed a handle each, stepping back to open the doors wide.

Freya sucked in a steadying breath as her eyes hungrily took in the details of the room. A four-poster bed set with golden drapes in an opulent room adorned with fine art and floor-to-ceiling windows. Gilt-edged tables, fresh flowers in vases that were almost as tall as she was.

And standing in the middle, in a long white tunic and trousers, was Jamie. As if he'd been waiting for her.

She stared at him, not sure what to do. Or say.

Now she could understand why he hadn't just told her all this.

'You're right,' she said, clearing her throat and looking straight at him. 'I would never have believed you.'

Jamie poured her some tea, adding two cubes of sugar to the drink. He frowned slightly when he saw how her hands were shaking when she went to take it from him, then set it down on the table instead and took her hands in his to calm them.

'It's all right, Freya.'

'Is it?' She looked at him askance. 'Who *are* you, Jamie?'

'My name is Jameel Al Bakhari and I am heir to the throne of Majidar. My older brother Ilias is King, ruling with his wife Queen Jasmeen, but they have been unable to sire any children so I am next in line. I also have a younger sister, Zahra, who has just married.'

It all sounded as if it was from a film. 'Heir to the throne…?'

'Yes.'

'Royalty?'

'Yes.'

It was a struggle to process. 'But…but you work as a midwife.'

'Yes.'

'Why? Why do that, when you're a…a prince?'

He smiled. 'I did not ask to be born a prince. Ruling a kingdom and waving at crowds from a distance is not what I felt I was meant to do. I want to *know* people. Help them personally. When my father sat upon the throne he took us with him to a hospital, where he was opening a new neonatal unit. I was very young—maybe eight or nine. We toured the labour ward, saw the new state-of-the-art theatre and the incubators that held tiny newborns. I was fascinated by the babies, and when we returned to the palace an idea took hold. The more I thought about it, the more I realised I wanted to deliver babies. To hold the miracle of life in my own two hands and experience the joy of bringing a new life into the world.'

Freya nodded. 'But why be a midwife? You could have been a doctor. An obstetrician. A surgeon!'

'I could. But those paths didn't interest me. I wanted to deliver the babies. An obstetrician gets called in only if there's a problem. A surgeon just takes care of Caesareans. I wanted to be there through the whole labour—to monitor progress, develop that close relationship a midwife creates with each patient. My mother spoke fondly of all her midwives. I would beg her to tell me, over and over again, the stories of our births—mine, my brother's and my sister's. Even after all those years she could remember every detail, and it was the midwives of whom she spoke the most highly. I wanted to be that person. To have that impact on people's lives. To be remembered in such a way. Selfish, perhaps, but true.'

'I don't think it's selfish.'

He inclined his head in thanks. 'I asked my father if I could study towards midwifery. Focus on the sciences so that midwifery could be my calling. But he would not allow it. He said it was not appropriate for a prince of my standing to attend to such work usually reserved for women.'

Freya couldn't imagine what she might have felt if her mother had forbidden her from becoming a midwife. 'What happened?'

'I had to put my wishes to one side until my father died and my brother Ilias took the throne. I assumed then, like they did, that they would soon overwhelm the palace with little babies and that I would no longer be next in line to sit upon the throne and rule. So I begged Ilias to let me come to England to follow my education and have the life that I wanted. Ilias is much more modern in his thinking and he agreed that I should have the life of my own choosing.'

'You said your brother doesn't have any children?'

'No. Ilias and Jasmeen have never been blessed. Therefore I am still next in line to sit on the throne—something I have no desire to do, but must endure when the time comes. And it *will* come. Eventually. My brother, as considerate as he is, has begun asking me when I will return. He tells me that I must be seen to be upholding some of my royal duties, so that when my time comes the people will know me better and accept my succession.'

'So you have to go back?'

'Not immediately. Ilias is still young—just a few years older than me—but his health is not the best.'

Freya looked down at her tea. The nausea and shock had subsided somewhat now, and she felt more comfortable about taking a sip. 'So what you're trying to say, in a roundabout way, is that I'm carrying the heir to your throne?'

Jamie inhaled a deep breath as he looked at her. She seemed tiny suddenly. He hadn't wanted to scare her, or overwhelm her, but he'd known if he'd tried to explain this on the hospital ward she would never have believed it. She needed to see it. Experience this.

'Yes.'

His acknowledgement was too much. Too

overwhelming. She suddenly felt as if she was being suffocated as her mind whirled with all the possibilities that would entail. She got up and began to pace. Walking back and forth, back and forth as she thought hard about how she could get out of this situation.

A royal baby? Heir to a throne? It would mean her life changing. Never to be hers again. All her choices taken from her. All her control gone and given over to someone else.

'Tradition dictates that if everything remains well we should marry before the child is born.'

What? Marriage? No, no, no, no...

She shook her head frantically. 'I'm sorry, but no. I can't. I can't do that, Jamie. I *won't*!'

He stood up too, and reached for her arm, but she swiped his hand away.

'Marrying you would make me...what? A princess? A *queen*? I can't be that! Stared at... With people judging me on a global scale... Why do you think I do night shifts? I love my little world. I'm happy there. I'm accepted. Do you think I want *any* of what you're offering?'

'But, Freya, we need to—'

It was all spiralling away. Her control—everything. Disappearing into a black hole that was vast and powerful. It couldn't happen. She wouldn't let it! She had the right to say no!

She didn't know this man. Even though she'd

been intimate with him, conceived a child with him, worked with him. She didn't know him.

Didn't know how he would react if she backed away…

Would he be like Mike? Refuse to let her go?

I need to get away.

Her hand reached into her bag and grasped her mobile phone. She pulled it out and activated the phone keypad, pressed the numbers nine-nine-nine and hesitated. Ready to press 'Call' if anything went wrong.

'No, Jamie. *We* don't need to do anything. *You* don't need to do anything. You can forget about me—you can walk away and pretend that I never existed. You can go back to your kingdom, when the time arrives, and marry a proper princess—someone beautiful, someone the people will expect.'

'You *are* beautiful.'

She laughed at his response. 'You're just saying that. Do you really think you would have asked a girl like me to marry you if I wasn't pregnant? With *this* face? I don't think so.'

He stood in front of her. 'Your face doesn't matter. You are a strong, beautiful woman.'

'Of course it matters. It's what people see! It's what they judge you on. I know this better than anyone. I appreciate that you're trying to say and do the right thing, but it's not the right thing for

Majidar. It's not the right thing for *me*. Your people don't need me by the side of their King. A one-night stand who got pregnant? A commoner from another country? *No*. I absolve you of all responsibility. Send me money each month, if that will make you feel better about it, but please, Jamie, I beg of you, walk away. It will be better for you if you just let me go.'

She was trying to sound reasonable. Trying to sound calm and steady so that he would remain so, too. Her thumb hovered over the 'Call' button. He hadn't seen the number she had keyed in and she appreciated that he was keeping his distance physically. But she would press it if she had to.

'I cannot. I *will* not.'

Freya sighed, her eyes filling with sorrow. 'I can't be who you need me to be. I can't live that sort of life. That's not who I am.'

'Neither am I. But it is my destiny. And now, because of the child, it is also yours.'

Freya closed her eyes as if she were in pain, and then she opened them again, looking at him with tears in her eyes, as if she were sorry to be causing such distress. Sorry to have to deny him.

She was afraid to say the next words, but knew she had to, so that he was clear on where she stood. 'No, Jamie. Never.'

And then she backed away. She yanked open

the large doors to his suite and hurried down the corridor, expecting at any moment that the guards would drag her back, her finger still hovering over the button on her phone.

But the guards simply followed her at a respectful distance.

The lift was waiting for her and she got in and punched the button for the ground floor. Only when the doors slid closed and she was safe inside did she clear the numbers and slip her phone back into her bag.

It had taken every ounce of her strength to refuse him. To say no and walk away, not knowing how he might react. The likelihood of him being like Mike was slim, but then she'd thought Mike was okay, too. And look at what had happened there.

As she ran across Reception and out into the cool morning air she hoped this meant it was all over. That he would not bother her again.

She had given him her answer.

He would do much better if he were to accept it.

CHAPTER THREE

SHE TRIED TO stay away from Jamie at work. She sensed he was giving her space, and she appreciated that, but she could tell by the way he looked at her from across the room that as far as *he* was concerned this was far from over.

There was no way she could accept his terms. *Marry* him? Become a princess, or whatever she would be? Have her child schooled to become a king or queen themselves? Living a life of privilege, no doubt, but one that would be like a prison. Never to pop to the shops when she wanted, go for a walk when she liked, without fearing that someone might get too close to the royal person...

It was ridiculous.

Her child wouldn't live like that. She wanted a normal life for her baby—a normal education, real friends, a real life and choices. She wanted to sit on the South Downs and have a picnic with her child. Fly a kite and take a dog for a walk. She wanted to walk barefoot on the beach and jump waves with him or her, laugh out loud and eat ice cream and fish and chips.

Normality.

It was the only thing she craved for her child. For herself. To live a normal life. Not the life that she had had since the attack, hiding from people and crowds. Not the childhood that Jamie had had, raised behind the walls of a palace. Something else. The childhood she'd had when she'd been growing up. When her face had been unspoilt by sulphuric acid—when her future had looked bright and the whole world had been a possibility.

Mike had limited her. Told her what she should wear, what she should eat, who she could talk to. And when he hadn't been able to control her, hadn't been able to keep her, he had tried to make sure that no one else would want her.

Saying no to Jamie had taken every ounce of bravery she had. But she wouldn't allow another man to control her, and Jamie's request demanded something of her that she couldn't give. Basically, it seemed to her that he wanted her whole life—her dedication, her child—to be given to him and his country. A country she had never even heard of just one week ago.

Jamie had a duty to his throne, but she didn't. Nor did their child. And she refused to tie either of them down to it.

* * *

A person's skin is made up of proteins. Protein makes up the structure of cells and the enzymes within them. Acid, when it comes into contact with protein, changes its innate structure and causes it to break down immediately upon contact. It's excruciating, the pain—difficult to relieve. The strongest medications often have no effect...

Freya sat in the hospital staffroom, waiting for her shift to start. Her mind was torturing her with the memory of that day so long ago, when her world had been turned upside down.

She'd tried to hold up her hands to protect her face, but it had been too late, and then suddenly—instantly—the terrifying scorching of her skin had begun.

She'd thought those screams were from other people, but they'd been her own. Freya had collapsed onto the pavement, her eyes squeezed tightly shut, afraid to open them in case she couldn't see, screaming at people to help her.

Some guy had tried pouring water over her face to dilute the acid, but it had simply run down her neck and begun burning her there, too.

It had seemed an age before the paramedics had arrived. Before the morphine had hit her veins, before they'd tried to irrigate her skin and whisked her to hospital.

Despite the burning she'd begun to feel cold. Shock, they said. Apparently, burns could cause hypothermia. Who knew?

It was a day she would never forget. And all because a man had refused to let her go.

She'd told Jamie no. She'd turned down his marriage proposal, refused to let him take her and the baby back to his country. How would he react now?

As if her worries had summoned him, Jamie entered the staffroom. His gaze met hers, briefly, and then he looked away.

What did that mean? Was he upset? Angry? Was he the type to seek revenge?

So far he seemed reasonable. Normal. A little sad, maybe, but nothing like Mike. But for how long? What about when he got called back to his country and the time came for him to leave? Would he put pressure on her then? Would he try to blackmail her? Threaten her?

She didn't want to tar him with the same brush as Mike, but her history with men so far had not been good. She couldn't read him yet. Didn't understand him. Perhaps if she remained polite and respectful he would remain that way too? Perhaps if she got to know him a little more she might understand him better?

But she was afraid to do that.

Getting to know him meant spending time with him...

Caroline Müller was well into her labour—contracting every two minutes, alternating between taking amusing selfies with her husband Stefan when she was between contractions, and breathing and retreating into herself when she was having pain, going all Zen, peaceful and in control.

It was a marvel to behold.

Freya was happy she could distract herself at work—the place where she could absorb herself in her patient's labour and just for a few hours forget about her own life.

'How are you doing, Caroline? Still coping?'

Caroline had requested no pain relief. She wanted to try and give birth naturally to her first child. Freya wanted to support her in that, but also to let her know that she could change her mind whenever she needed to.

'I'm good, I think.' Her patient nodded, as if she were reassuring herself that she could do this. 'Do you think I'm doing okay?'

Freya smiled. 'You're coping wonderfully. Eight centimetres dilated and still no pain relief! You're a marvel.'

Freya was very keen on honouring a woman's

choice. Of all the things in the world a woman could do, going through labour and childbirth was an extremely personal thing. No one else could do it for her. She was on her own. Pulling on the resources and reserves that only she had within her own body.

It was an eye-opening and eye-watering experience. No one could know how they would cope with those levels of pain. And if a mother wanted to give birth without pain relief or with every medication going then Freya would support her either way. Childbirth wasn't a competition, and the mother alone was the one who must decide her course of treatment. It was important to empower a woman with the knowledge that any choice over her body was her own.

Caroline blew out a breath and nodded. 'Thanks. Did you know Stefan's mother wanted to be here at the birth?'

Freya looked at Stefan. 'I didn't.'

'I told her she wasn't welcome—which didn't go down very well. I didn't want my own mother here, so there was no way I was having my in-laws loitering around my nether regions.'

Freya and Stefan smiled at each other.

'My mother can be quite controlling,' he said. 'This is her first grandchild and we've had to be quite firm with her about not booking things in advance.'

'What sort of things?'

'Enrolling him or her in a private nursery, hiring a nanny, booking her personal swimming instructor to give our newborn swimming lessons, *and* pre-book a German teacher so that our child will grow up to be bilingual. German is my mother's natural tongue,' he explained, smiling with amusement.

'Wow!' Freya mused. 'She sounds wonderfully keen to provide your little one with the very best.'

'She has to be reined in or she doesn't know when to stop!' Caroline said, and grimaced as another contraction began to build.

She closed her eyes, relaxed her brow and began to breathe steadily in through her nose and then slowly and smoothly out through her mouth. She stood to one side of the bed, leaning on the mattress, swaying her hips from side to side as the contraction intensified.

'That's it, Caroline, you're doing really well. Keep breathing.'

Freya rubbed the small of her patient's back, wondering how royal families raised their babies.

Weren't they all surrounded by nannies? Whisked off to nurseries and only brought to their parents to hold when they were clean and fed and presentable?

Actually, she had no idea how royals looked

after a new baby. Nor did she have any idea about a desert kingdom's culture.

But what she *did* know was that she didn't want her child to be taken away from her. This was *her* baby and she wanted to raise it. With Jamie's help, if he wanted, but she would have the final say in everything.

There would be no taking the baby away to a nursery at night time. She wanted to deal with midnight feeds and nappy explosions. She wanted to soothe her baby when it started to teethe. She wanted to be the one who took her child to the doctor for vaccinations and check-ups, to comfort it when it cried because some stranger had poked at it with a needle or a stethoscope.

Was it too much to ask? This might be Jamie's baby too, and he might come from a royal line of kings, but it was also *her* baby and she *wasn't* royal. She was normal—girl-next-door. And she wanted her child to have a normal life.

Caroline began to groan out loud—thick guttural noises coming from deep within her. 'Oh, I think I want to push!'

'Try not to. Not just yet. I need to check you again…make sure you're fully dilated.'

She was. With a wide smile she informed Caroline that with the next contraction she could start pushing, and that hopefully, within the next hour, they would have their longed-for baby.

'Will I really?' Caroline began to cry. Happy tears springing from her eyes as she reached for her husband's hand, clutching it tightly.

He squeezed back. 'We will.'

Caroline wanted to remain standing between contractions, and then lowered herself into a crouch beside by the bed each time she pushed. She pushed long and hard, her face reddening, sweat pouring down with her efforts, until after about forty minutes she began to crown.

'You're nearly there now!' Freya watched intently and quietly as Caroline gave birth to the baby's head. It had thick black hair and Caroline reached down to touch.

'My baby!' she cried.

'One final push, Caroline! You can do this!'

Freya supported the baby with her gloved hands as it was delivered, and then passed the crying baby over to its mother, who lifted her up from between her legs to cradle her against her chest.

'Oh, my God! It's a girl! We have a little girl, Stefan!'

Freya clamped the cord and Stefan cut it, and then she helped guide the new mum onto the bed, so she could rest whilst Freya took care of all the little things that needed doing. The syntocinon.

Checking to see if mum needed stitches. For any sign of haemorrhage.

She draped a couple of towels around the baby to help keep it warm as Caroline placed her daughter against her skin beneath her hospital gown. Then Freya checked the placenta to make sure it was complete and healthy.

After she'd written the pertinent times and details into her patient's file, she took the baby to weigh it and check its APGAR score—the scale against which all newborn babies were measured to ensure they were coping with life outside of the womb.

Handing the baby back for more skin-to-skin, she asked if Caroline and Stefan had chosen a name yet?

'Hannah Rose.'

'That's beautiful,' she said.

'Thank you. Thank you for everything, Freya—we really mean it. We couldn't have done it without you.'

She smiled her thanks. 'I couldn't have done it, without you! I'll leave you on your own for a little while. Press the buzzer if you need me, but I'll be back to take you down to the postnatal ward.'

She left the new parents to it—Stefan already taking pictures with his phone—and quietly closed the door behind her. Then, carrying her patient's notes, she headed over to the desk and sat down.

Freya was hungry…thirsty. She hadn't had anything for hours, having stayed with her patient for most of the night, popping out only once to use the toilet because her bladder had threatened to explode if she didn't.

Mona came out of the small kitchenette, carrying a tray filled with mugs of tea. 'Ah! Perfect timing. Want one?'

'Ooh, yes, please!' Freya grabbed a hot mug and gratefully took a sip. 'My patient just delivered a baby girl—Hannah Rose. Isn't that a beautiful name?'

'Gorgeous! How did she get through it?'

'Not a single scrap of pain medication!' Freya stated proudly.

'Good for her! I have no pain threshold whatsoever. I practically needed an epidural for a tiny blister I got on my heel. What about you?' Then Mona's face darkened as she realised what she'd said. 'Sorry…'

But Freya wasn't offended. Mona was her closest friend here, and she knew she hadn't meant anything nasty by it.

Freya thought back to her days spent in hospital after the acid attack. The pain she'd been in. The pain she'd had to live through for months as her face recovered. The nightmares. The flashbacks. The searing, agonising torture of debride-ment. She'd had enough pain for one lifetime.

She smiled. 'I want everything they can give me.'

Jamie had been watching her carefully over the last few weeks. As much as he could, anyway. Clearly she was trying to avoid being with him. He kept catching her noticing him arrive in the staffroom or at the reception desk and suddenly getting that *I'm busy* look before she got up to go and do something.

He was finding it terribly frustrating when all he wanted to do was talk to her. Find out how she was. Whether she was feeling okay. She had to be due for the first scan of the baby any day now, but she'd made no mention of it to him and he didn't want to miss it. Nor did he like this dis-tance she was creating between them, as if she didn't want him involved, because that was not how he planned to have his first child. Being cast aside as if he was just a sperm donor.

Having a baby was one of the most wonderful things a woman could do. To become a parent one of the most rewarding privileges. He really hoped that Freya would thaw towards him, but he could understand why she hadn't yet.

Mona had told him what had happened to her years ago. Some possessive ex had thrown acid in her face. The very idea of that made him feel sick. It caused a rage to build in him towards a man he knew was already in prison.

Mona hadn't said much else, clearly reluctant to gossip about her friend, but he'd had to ask. He'd spent so many nights wondering why she was keeping him at such a distance. Why she seemed so edgy and uncomfortable. Why she kept looking at him as if he was some firework that might go off at any minute. It had made him wonder what had happened to her. And now he knew.

Freya MacFadden was having a strange effect on him. She was so petite, so dainty, and he loved seeing her walk in with her long blonde hair hanging loose down her back, watching her scoop it up, twist it and pin it into place each shift. It was an action so casually done, without looking in a mirror, and she always managed a tousled look which, with those big blue eyes of hers, was a winning combination.

The scars didn't bother him at all. Not like that. What bothered him about them was that someone had done that to her. Intentionally. That she had suffered, and that her life had been changed for evermore. He'd visited clinics that cared for women attacked like this, and he'd never seen such suffering before or since. It was a memory that haunted him, but he'd learnt something from those women—that they had tremendous courage. That they bore a bravery within them that he could never hope to emulate.

Freya was the same.

He was worried that she didn't seem to be letting him in, but he understood why and knew that he would have to bide his time if she were to trust him.

He leaned against her locker, straightening when he heard her coming down the corridor, chatting to Mona. He hoped to end this stalemate between them—to get them talking again. Ask her how she was…if she needed anything.

He saw her notice him. Watched as she debated whether to avoid using her locker after all. But then she seemed to overcome that hesitation and came over to him.

'Excuse me, I need to get inside.'

He stepped back, giving her space. 'Could we talk for a moment?'

She looked up at him hesitantly. 'About what?'

'About us.'

'There is no "us".' She glanced over at their colleagues, afraid of being overheard. But no one appeared to be listening.

She shoved her bag into her locker and hung up her coat. Then she did the hair thing that he loved and clipped her ID badge to her uniform.

'Can you tell me if you're feeling okay? If there's anything I can do?'

'I'm feeling fine. A bit sick, but eating often seems to help.'

He could see in her face that she was still closed off from him. Unwilling to share. He understood that, and he was willing to wait.

'Well, if there's anything I can do for you then please let me know.'

She nodded and bit her lip.

'Can I get you a tea? A coffee?'

She glanced over at their friends by the kettle and the sink. 'No, but thank you.'

'Have you told anyone?'

Her eyes darkened. 'No. Not yet. Have you?'

He shook his head. 'No.'

'Right. What will happen when you do?'

He imagined the reaction of his family. They would be insistent upon marriage. They would be insistent about him coming home and building his life as a father and future King of Majidar.

'They'll be delighted.'

Her eyes narrowed, as if she were trying to assess him for the truth. *'Right.'*

'Oh, I brought you these.' From behind his back he drew out a brown paper bag filled with grapes. 'As promised.'

A small smile *almost* broke out across her

face, but she checked it and instead frowned. 'I'm not sick.'

'No, I know.'

'You don't have to do this…' she whispered.

He nodded and whispered back, 'I do. So if you need anything—*anything*—I hope you will ask me.'

And he left her at her locker to go and grab himself a drink.

Little inroads…small kindnesses. That was what she needed. He needed to build her trust. He needed to show her that he could be relied upon to look out for her and keep her safe. She needed to see that he was everything that the man who'd attacked her was not. That he believed in kindness and respect and love. That he believed in honour and duty and that he would shirk neither.

Baby steps.

The next shift they had together Freya nodded her head towards him, as if to say *good morning*. The one after that she actually said hello.

Jamie gave her more space and time.

One night shift she came in and straight away headed for the staff toilet, emerging fifteen minutes later looking a little green. He presented her with ginger tea—something that his mother had sworn by. Another time when she looked queasy and was meant to check on a patient in Postnatal, he offered to answer the call bell instead.

Where he could, he took the time to try and lighten her load. To make it easier for her whilst she was going through this difficult time.

Their colleagues had begun to suspect that something was up, and Mona had been the one to ask Freya during a night shift.

'Are you *pregnant*?'

Clearly Freya had realised it was pointless to try and deny it. Not when the signs were so obvious and she was surrounded by people who specialised in pregnancy and babies.

The team had been delighted! Hugging her and congratulating her.

'Who's the father?'

Freya had baulked at answering, but she had looked at him, as if to give him permission to answer.

He'd stepped forward. 'I am.'

Well, that had sent the gossip mill into high speed!

He had seen that Freya wasn't overly happy about being the centre of attention, but she'd seemed to cope with it—probably because these were her friends and people she trusted.

After that everyone had tried their best to help

Freya out whilst the morning sickness was so devastating. She really was suffering, poor thing.

'Are you guys, like, together?' Mona had asked him.

Jamie had longed to say *Not yet*, but had felt that would be pushing too far, before Freya was ready. This was not a world in which two people could be forced into marriage. It was not something that had been arranged since they were children. It was not a unification of two countries solidifying a pact by marrying off a prince and princess.

This was real life. Freya was a commoner. A woman from the west. She had different expectations from life and a whole lot of baggage that she needed to sift through before she realised he was a good guy.

'Your first scan should be soon,' he said as he brought her another cup of ginger tea one day.

'It is.'

'I was wondering…only if you feel right about it…if I might come with you?'

She looked at him carefully, almost as if she were appraising him. She'd been giving him this look a lot just lately.

'Okay.'

His heart almost burst with joy. *'Okay?'*

'Sure. It's your baby too.'

'Thank you, Freya!'

He almost imploded with excitement, but managed to contain himself. Strong emotions, sudden reactions, were not the kind of thing that would make Freya feel safe. She needed to see that he was stable, even if his insides were fizzing with glee and he wanted to jump about and yell for all the world to hear.

They sat together, waiting for the ultrasound technician to call Freya's name.

She felt uncomfortable. Not just because she'd had to drink a huge amount of water beforehand, and hold it in, but also because she was back in what she considered the 'normal' world. Daylight hours. Where there were too many people about. People who, she noticed, kept glancing at her, trying to work out what was different about her. Noticing her face...

Part of her wanted to stare back at them. Challenge them with a single raised eyebrow as if to ask, *What are you looking at?* But she wasn't brave enough or rude enough.

Freya had been raised to show respect to people. To be polite and to treat others the way she wished to be treated herself. She couldn't do that to strangers. They didn't deserve it. They were just being curious. It was human nature to take a second look at something that didn't quite fit.

She wondered how many of them were wondering how on earth she could be sitting there with this gorgeous man next to her.

Jamie clearly had no idea of his allure. Ink-dark hair, midnight eyes that penetrated the soul, and a bearing that screamed royalty—due, no doubt, to a childhood that had consisted of years of being told to sit up straight, shoulders back. Not to slouch. To meet people's eyes. Assess the situation. Listen. Look commanding.

She felt tiny next to him. Inconsequential. He was so tall, proud and strong, and she was small, scarred and nauseous.

How much of her feeling sick was due to the pregnancy, though? Her stress levels were high. She dreaded to think what her blood pressure was. But she had to admit she wouldn't have got through these last few weeks of her first trimester without Jamie's help.

He had been instrumental in getting her through it, and she'd quickly come to realise that she had begun to rely on him being close. Always there with a hot, steaming mug of ginger tea, or some peppermints, or one of the strawberry milkshakes which she had begun craving. Whatever she'd needed—a rest, a moment to herself, someone to take care of her patients whilst she clutched the toilet bowl—he'd provided it. Her friends, too, yes. But Jamie had been the most considerate and for that she was grateful.

And scared.

He was getting under her skin. She was beginning to like him. Once she'd come on shift and, when she'd realised that he wasn't rostered on with her, a huge sense of disappointment and loss had hit her like a brick.

How had that happened?

She never wanted to rely on a man again.

And yet here she was. Not only was she tied to this man but he was also a prince, he had a duty, and she was refusing to accept that. She knew she must somehow be tearing him in two. He had a duty to his country. To his people.

I'm hurting him and yet he doesn't complain.

They didn't look right together—no wonder people were staring. She was just a girl. A scarred, damaged girl. And he... Well, Jamie was something else entirely, and he deserved a beautiful princess to stand by his side and make pretty babies with him.

'Freya MacFadden?'

She straightened, rising to her feet. Behind her, she felt Jamie stand and follow her into the darkened room.

They went through the preliminaries with the technician. Date of last period, how many weeks pregnant she was, whether she felt well.

Frightened, she lay down, not sure what was scaring her more—the prospect of seeing her baby on screen, at last, or the fact that she wanted Jamie at her side. She'd anticipated doing this alone. Not telling him. Sneaking in to the appointment after everyone on the night shift had gone and having this moment all to herself. Knowing she would cry. Knowing she would get emotional because finally, *finally* this day had come. The day she would see irrefutable proof that she was pregnant. With a baby she'd thought she would never have.

The technician squirted the gel and applied the probe to Freya's abdomen.

Freya bit her lip. She might have got this all wrong. Perhaps she wasn't even pregnant at all? A false positive? A molar pregnancy? Then everyone could go back to their normal lives. Jamie could leave and go on to another post, or back to his country, and she could remain unchanged on the night shift, revelling in the joy of other people's babies and just imagining what it might feel like to hold her own baby...

The technician was smiling. 'Everything looks wonderful here.'

Freya let out a breath she hadn't realised she'd been holding. 'Really?'

'Any history of multiples in either family?'

What?

The technician turned the screen so that Freya and Jamie could see. There, in black and white, was her womb. Filled with not one but *two* babies, separated by a very fine line which meant…

'Twins? Non-identical twins?' Jamie stared at the screen, laughing with shock and delight.

Freya had to remind herself to breathe. She couldn't quite believe it! Twins? Her grandmother had been one of a pair of twins, but she'd never imagined that this would happen to her. 'Oh, my God…'

'Freya, can you believe it?' Jamie scooped up her hand in his and kissed it, his dark eyes sparkling with unshed tears in the shadows of the room.

She stared at him, seeing his joy, his beaming face, his eyes twinkling in the semi-darkness of the room.

She felt her body flooding with adrenaline. *Twins.* Non-identical twins.

This was crazy. Unbelievable! It was…

She stared at the screen once again. Counted again. Two babies. Growing inside her.

Two.

'I don't believe it.'

The technician continued to make her checks. Measuring the babies, the length of their femurs, checking the Nuchal fold at the backs of their necks.

'Your babies look beautiful. Perfectly healthy and a good size. It probably accounts for all that morning sickness you've been having. You'll get more scans and check-ups due to this being a twin pregnancy, so if you have any problems don't hesitate to shout.' She smiled at them both. 'You ought to go and celebrate.'

Perhaps. But Freya didn't foresee having a party. She liked the idea of keeping it quiet. Just telling family and the people at work. They were the only people she knew anyway.

Jamie probably had loads of people he needed to tell. His family. His staff. His advisors. What would they all tell him to do? He couldn't walk away now, could he? She was carrying *two* royal children.

If she hadn't felt trapped before, she most definitely felt it now.

She began to hyperventilate and felt Jamie's fingers wrap around her own.

'It's okay, Freya. Just breathe slowly. In and out. That's it, slow your breathing.'

She focused on his face. On his voice. On him, her only connection to this world. She felt spaced out, as if she was adrift in a vast universe and he was the umbilical cord connecting her to reality.

He had intensely dark eyes. Eyes she could lose herself in. She had once before and now she needed to again.

Was she about to get swept up into a load of

royal political intrigue? Be married and whisked away to live in a desert? Something like that?

How could she continue to live the private life that she loved? Was she about to lose all control over her every decision? Because she wasn't sure she could do that.

This life, her *babies'* lives, were too important. Jamie's demands were not more important than her own.

She'd lost all control once. Had all decisions taken from her. She had lived a life trapped in a hospital, in pain and afraid, with staff all around her, checking on her every hour of the day, waiting on her hand and foot. It had been unbearable. Living a half-life, staring out of windows, watching the world go by and wishing she could be in it. Wishing that the pain would go away, so she could escape...

I won't have that happen again.

Slowly her breathing came back under her control. Jamie was smiling at her, with relief on his face that she was calming down. Sitting up, she pulled her hand from his. She had relied on him enough.

'I'm okay. I'm all right.'

The sonographer passed her a couple of scan pictures. 'Twins can be a bit of a shock. It might take some time to get used to.'

Jamie was watching her, assessing her. He offered her his hand, so she could get up off the bed, but she did it without his help.

She couldn't keep relying on him. He had other commitments. Other duties. No matter what he said their lives were incompatible, and no matter how much she might want something else she couldn't have him and he couldn't have her.

I just need to keep telling myself that.

The rush hour traffic was building around the hospital. The car park was filling with vehicles. Staff were arriving, visitors…

Freya pulled up the collar of her jacket and adjusted her scarf. Aware of too many pairs of eyes all around her.

Jamie stood beside her, gazing down at the scan pictures the technician had given them.

'This doesn't change anything,' she said, hoisting her bag strap firmly into place on her shoulder.

'No?'

'No.'

He stared back at her, frowning, a small divot forming between his dark brows. 'There must be something I can do. To make this easier for you.'

Why did he have to have such a beautiful voice? Deep, slightly accented, smooth and delightful. He was already handsome and charming. Helpful and kind. Did he have to be sexy, too? Couldn't the man have one single fault?

He does. He's royal.

She was struggling not to cry again. Her hormones washed through her with renewed force now that she knew she was carrying twins.

'You could leave. Get a contract someplace else.'

'That's never going to happen. You think I'm going to walk away from you? All three of you?'

With eyes blurred from unshed tears, she glanced up at him and then away as she headed for her car to go home.

'You're under no obligation to be with me, Jamie. I told you that. Why can't you just go? Pretend this never happened? I'll never ask anything of you.'

She heard his footsteps as he hurried to catch up with her. Felt his hand upon her arm, turning her.

'I'm *never* walking away from you. You need to stop asking me to do that.'

She wasn't sure she could do this. How had she got herself into another situation where a man was refusing to let her go? Demanding to stay in her life? It was scary. She didn't want it. *Any* of it! She just wanted to be left in peace. To deal with this alone. Why couldn't she be living her happy dream? The one where she was married and was about to have a family with the man she loved and who loved her and where everything was normal and light and easy? And not terrifying.

'Jamie, I can't be who you need me to be.'

'Who do you think I need?'

'A princess. A queen. A *wife*. Someone who can stand by your side proudly. Someone who can wave to cheering crowds. Someone who can be loved by your people.'

'They'd love any woman I chose to have by my side.'

'Because of their duty?'

'Yes.'

'I don't want love out of *duty*, Jamie. And I could never stand beside you like that. I could never live away from my family. My job. My life. My life and my babies' lives will be *here*. Not in Majidar. You need to accept that.'

She pointed her key fob at her car to unlock it and opened the door.

'You *will* be called at some point to take your brother's throne and be King, so leave me now, leave *us* now and then no one will have to get hurt.' She got in, closed the car door shut after her and gave him one last look.

Did he not understand how much this was hurting *her*? She'd dreamed of this day! She'd never imagined she would ever be blessed by one baby, never mind two, but in that dream of having babies she'd hoped to have a wonderful man by her side too. In her imagination he'd always been a tall, dark and handsome figure, his face blurred. She'd never been sure who he might be. She'd dreamt of a family. Her children, her husband.

Mike had taken that dream away from her the second he'd thrown that acid, but now it was within her grasp again. And it was all wrong.

She wished she could develop something with Jamie, but he had another calling, apart from midwifery.

He was going to be King.

And she could not leave everything and everyone she knew to live her life beside him. A life of publicity, of always having her photograph taken, with her every choice of clothing or hairstyle criticised and appraised. Her face discussed and talked about in newspapers and on television channels, her relationship with Mike dredged up from history, where she'd consigned it. They'd no doubt track him down in prison, interview him, get the inside scoop on their relationship and publish that too.

A life with Jamie would mean a lifetime of judgement.

All she'd ever wanted was to be loved.

And love did not come from duty.

Jamie pressed his hands against her window and begged her to lower it so he could speak.

She dropped the window slightly and the coolness of the outside air filtered into the car's interior.

Jamie stared at her. 'People are already hurting, Freya. You are. I am. We need to work together to sort this—not just for us, but for our children.'

Her hands went to her belly, protectively wrapping around them. 'They're who I'm thinking of.'

His eyes had narrowed slightly and frustration crept into his voice. '*Are* you, Freya? Or are you just thinking of the man who did that to you? Letting his actions dictate how you think your life must be?'

She bit her lip. Because he was right. Mike—his actions years ago, his attack, her fear—was being allowed to run every decision she made.

But who was Jamie to think he could tell her this? Say it? Confront her with it? As if he had the right?

'I'm their father, Freya. Let me be with my children!'

CHAPTER FOUR

WALK AWAY AND no one would get hurt? Did she think he was made of stone? He already had feelings about this. About the babies. About *her*.

Freya didn't seem to understand that.

He was *already* involved. Already in too deep and he always would be—until the day he took his last breath. These were his *children*!

And she…she was *scared*.

He understood that. What she'd been through… He couldn't even begin to imagine *half* the pain she must have experienced. She must have thought her life was over. Her face ruined. Her life destroyed by what had happened. Had she believed she didn't have a future?

All he wanted to do was help her feel safe. Make sure she was all right. But she seemed determined to keep pushing him away. It was very frustrating and he was trying his hardest not to make demands.

She truly was remarkable. He had nothing but

admiration for her. Her spirit, her bravery made her shine from within. She didn't understand that. She didn't realise just how much people cared for her because of who she was. She believed they judged her purely on what she looked like.

She was still beautiful. Imperfections on her face meant nothing. It was who someone was that made them attractive.

Clearly Freya was still bothered by her face and he understood that. Women today were bombarded with messages about what constituted beauty, and it was all focused on outward appearances—being model-thin, having long, luscious hair, drop-dead gorgeous features. Beauty was never seen in acts of charity, or kindness, or caring. No one was ever told that having a good, loving heart was beautiful.

So he would protect her. Care for her as much as she would let him. And hopefully she would begin to let down her walls. To trust him.

He tried to make sure she always had a drink or a snack, as she kept staying in her patients' rooms and not coming out for a break, and he couldn't allow that. She needed to keep her strength up. But when he did these things for her she would give him a look that was almost like fear. As if she was worried about what he might do next. A look that said *You really don't have to do this.*

But he did. Whether she liked it or not they were joined now. For evermore. With or without rings on their fingers.

He brought her mugs of tea. He'd even offered to massage her aching feet once, when she'd complained about them, but all she'd done in response was look at him as if he was mad and then she'd got up to go and do something else. When she should have been resting!

She wouldn't let him in. Wouldn't let him get close.

His security people had told him that after she left the hospital and went home she stayed in. Never went anywhere. Didn't seem to have a life. There had been one visit, where she'd gone to someone's house, but a quick background check had discovered that it was her mother's home. He'd debated about calling in, hoping to meet her mother, but had refrained, not knowing how she'd react to that. If she thought his making her a cup of tea at work was bad, he felt sure she wouldn't want him pushing into her life before he was invited.

The security detail he'd assigned to her reported in every day. It broke his heart that she lived such an isolated life. Was there some way in which he could help her to open up her world?

Or perhaps she was happy? Perhaps she was an introvert who enjoyed her own company? He wasn't in any position to judge.

'Would you like to meet me for coffee one day?' he asked her during a break on the ward.

She looked at him askance. 'Why? I see you every day at work.'

He smiled. 'It's different at work. We don't really get a chance to talk. We should be getting to know one another a bit more. We could meet in the open somewhere. In a public place, if that will make you feel better.'

He thought he was suggesting a *good* thing. Neutrality. Safety and security in numbers.

'I was attacked in a public place, Jamie. Surrounded by people. Numbers don't always make you safer.'

No. Of course not. He should have considered that. Freya liked privacy and quietness. She liked being alone.

'Chichester Cathedral.'

She frowned. 'What?'

'Let's meet at Chichester Cathedral. It's quiet, not too many people. There's a place to get coffee. Some grounds to wander in where we could find a private nook.'

'Because you want to talk?'

'Because we *need* to talk. Please, Freya, I beg of you.'

She seemed to consider his proposal. A divot formed in her brow. 'It's still too public for me.'

'Then where? Name it and I will arrange it.'

She thought of her bolthole on Hayling Island. The place she'd gone to after the attack. Her sanctuary.

'There's a path called the Billy Trail on Hayling Island. It starts just after the bridge to the mainland, on your right. We could meet there. I'll bring Rebel.'

Now it was his turn to frown. 'Who's Rebel?'

'My mother's dog.'

He wasn't the biggest fan of dogs, but he could get past that if she could get past her fears. 'Okay. When?'

It was Sunday afternoon, and the sun was burning down through a pure blue sky. He'd had to have the air-conditioning put on full when he'd got into the car because it was so hot. But he was glad the weather was good. He thought that if it had been raining, or bad weather in some way, Freya would have cancelled and they *needed* this. This time together. They needed to know more about one another. More beyond work and pregnancy and past horrors.

He and Freya were from vastly different backgrounds. It was no wonder they were clashing.

But they both had the same desire and that was to do the best thing for their babies.

His driver located the small car park just past the bridge. He'd never been this way before, and he'd been positively delighted at the beautiful harbours the bridge had driven them through. The soft stillness of the calm water, the white boats sitting on the surface, the stretch of coastline and beyond, across the water, the views to Portsmouth and the spire of the Spinnaker Tower.

He stood waiting for her to arrive and pretty soon saw her small car turn into the car park. He gave her a smile and a wave. He had butterflies in his stomach! He so wanted this meeting to go well between them. It was imperative that it did so.

His nerves grew worse when he saw her let a large German Shepherd dog out of the boot of her car. For some reason he'd expected something smaller, but Rebel was massive! He was dark with intense eyes, his ears up and alert, ready to protect his mistress.

His mouth dry, he began to walk towards them.

'Hi.'

He stopped, looking down at the dog. Rebel was panting from the heat, but all Jamie could see were rows of sharp white teeth.

Freya had him on a short leash. 'Rebel, sit.'

Instantly the dog sat and looked up to her, waiting for the next order.

He was impressed, but also trying to control the feeling that he needed to bolt. He desperately wanted to run away from this dog, but he had no doubt that it would run after him and pull him to the ground with a well-placed jaw around his arm or leg. Or somewhere worse!

'Are you okay?' she asked.

'Bit nervous of dogs, to be honest.'

She smiled, amused. 'Rebel's all right. You can trust him.'

'Does he know he can trust *me*?'

Her smile broadened. 'We're both still trying to work that out. So, shall we get going?' She slung a backpack over her shoulder and locked her car.

'Sure. How…um…how close should I get to you?'

'Beside me is fine. Don't worry, he won't rip your throat out unless I tell him to.'

'Oh, good. That makes me feel a lot better.'

She laughed. 'Come on!'

Clearly Freya felt at ease with the dog at her side, and he had to admit he really rather liked this relaxed Freya. The dog? Not so much.

Freya looked relaxed in her white tee shirt and blue shorts, sunglasses over her eyes and her hair swept back in a ponytail. She looked fresh and happy, and already he could see a slight swelling to her abdomen. Only three months pregnant, maybe, but this was twins so she was slightly bigger than normal.

Three or four people on mountain bikes went cycling past as they headed onto the path.

'You found the place all right, then?' she asked.

'My driver did.'

'Of course. You have servants. I forget that when I see you at work.'

'Just a driver. Some security. A valet at the hotel. Not much.'

'Not much, huh? You have the entire third floor. I think you have plenty.'

'Just a security issue, that's all.'

'Where are your guards today? Are they lurking behind bushes on the trail? Are they going to walk behind us at twenty paces?' She looked behind them, as if to check.

'Nothing like that.'

He didn't tell her that his security team had already swept the entire five-mile length of the trail. That he had one or two undercover men posing as walkers and another pretending to be a wildlife photographer. The trail passed a nature reserve, so it was the perfect place to hide men in plain sight.

'It must be hard to live a life that's watched over like that.'

'You tell *me*.'

She frowned. 'What do you mean?'

'Don't you think that everyone is constantly looking at *you*? Watching your every move?'

She looked away. 'That's different. That's a perception. Your life is a reality. One you can't escape from.'

'Is that why you don't want to be a part of it? Because people are always watching? Observing? Making judgements?'

'Partly.'

At least she was being honest.

'You don't notice it after a while,' he said.

'I would. I notice everything. Every little glance. Every raise of an eyebrow. Every frown. Every reaction—shock, fear, disgust. That last one I get more than you'd realise. Have you ever thought what that might feel like? To observe someone looking at your face and see that they're disgusted? Of course you haven't. Not looking the way you do. The world is open to those who are good-looking. It's a proven scientific fact. Beautiful and handsome people get better jobs, better pay, more opportunities. Disabled and disfigured people always seem to be at the bottom of the pile.'

'Life must have been hard for you.'

'Must have been? It still is.'

He didn't know how to answer that. He would never know exactly what she had been through. What she still went through, looking in the mirror and seeing a different face.

'But a new phase of our lives is opening up to both of us now.'

She nodded, stopping as Rebel bent his head to sniff at a small post in the ground. 'We have two separate, completely incompatible lives, Jamie. How are we going to manage this?'

The truth? He didn't know. He wanted to be a father to these babies, and to be in their lives, but he would be called upon to rule Majidar at some point and would have to leave this country. He didn't want to leave them behind and she refused to go with him.

He *loved* Majidar. Even though he had left it to come to England and make his life there. It was still his home. It was still the place where his family was. Where his heart was. His people were gracious and kind and understanding, but would they understand when they learned that he had left his children behind? Because he wouldn't. He couldn't get his head around it.

He loved these babies. Already. He'd seen their little hearts beating, had seen them in her womb, two gorgeous little beans that were *his*. He felt he would die for them. Lay down his life for them.

Already he dreamed of holding them in his arms, teaching them, playing with them, laughing at their chuckles and watching them grow.

Be a king. Or be a father.

It seemed to be one or the other, and it was an impossible decision to make.

'We *must* manage it. We must find a way.'

'But how?'

He smiled at her. 'Today is a good step forward. We can't afford to shut each other out; we don't have that luxury. I know it's hard for you—hard for you to trust me and let me in.' He paused over his next words, but knew he had to let her know that he *knew*. 'I know what happened to you.'

Freya stopped walking. So did Rebel, who turned back to look at her. 'Who told you?'

'No one was gossiping. I asked. I brought it up. I needed to know why you were shutting me out.'

She started walking again, Rebel loping by her side. 'I see.'

'I don't want you to be frightened of me, Freya. I'm not that kind of man.'

'I can't tell any more. My perspective on men is skewed.'

'Hence the big dog?' He smiled.

She glanced at him. 'Tell me why you're afraid of dogs.'

He thought about why he was afraid, glancing at Rebel's teeth. 'My brother and I were once playing out on the sand dunes. We'd gone out with our father, who was hunting with his falcons and his dogs. We had these big boards—like surfboards—and if we threw them right down the sloping side of a dune we could jump on and surf to the bottom. We were doing that… laughing and joking…having a brilliant time. I'd jumped onto my board and was sitting on it, surfing down the dune, when one of the dogs must have had his hunting instincts activated by our movement and high-pitched cries. This dog—this hound that was almost as tall as I was—raced over to me, and when the board stopped moving it grabbed onto my head, sinking its teeth into my scalp.'

Freya looked fascinated. Interested.

'My father got the dog to stop. It let go and I was rushed to the hospital with four puncture wounds to my skull. After that I couldn't go near any dogs. They made me too nervous.'

She nodded. 'So you know how it feels.'

He looked at her. 'I do. I know you don't know me well enough to be sure I'm not going to pounce, not going to sink my teeth in, but all I can say is I'm not like the man that did this to you. Just like Rebel, there, is probably nothing like the dog that attacked me.'

'You have to trust that.'

'As do you.'

He touched her on the arm, making her stop. Then he sucked in a breath as he contemplated what he had to do. Show her that if he was willing to work past his fear, then so should she. With some hesitation he held his hand out towards Rebel, hoping the dog wouldn't sense his fear. Hoping he wasn't about to lose a chunk of his hand. His heart racing, he watching in horrid fascination as Rebel licked his fingers, then began sniffing the cuff of his shirt.

Jamie knelt down in front of the dog and reached out to stroke it. His arms were trembling, but he was determined to do this. Rebel's fur was soft and thick and, most surprisingly, the dog didn't seem to mind him at all. Slowly he stood up and breathed a sigh of relief, a smile breaking across his face.

'Well, that went better than I'd imagined.'

A small smile broke across her face. 'That must have taken a lot of courage. Were you really that scared?'

'Terrified. But I trusted that I'd be okay. I hope you can do the same with me. Because only then can we get through this. As equals.'

They began walking again, side by side, enjoying the views over the harbour and its old oyster beds, where masses of birds were nesting.

'I'll try. That's all I can do.'

Jamie nodded. 'It's all I ask.'

Freya looked about her, then sucked in a breath and began talking. 'I guess I ought to tell you about him. About Mike—the guy that did this.'

'Only if you want to.'

'I do.'

Freya stooped to undo the clip on Rebel's lead and set him free.

Jamie felt a surge of anxiety, but decided he had to stay calm. She still had control of the dog. And the way the dog kept looking at her, waiting for instruction, showed that she did.

'Mike made me think we were equals. At the beginning. He seemed to adore me. Wanted to be with me all the time. I thought that was just so wonderful, you know? But over time it became insidious, the way he manipulated that. He made me feel bad about going out to see other people. He questioned my clothing. He wanted to know why I needed to wear make-up. Was it for someone else? Was I flirting? I tried to prove him wrong by not wearing make-up, but then he wanted me to cut my hair short. Said it made me look flirty, being so long, that men looked at women with long hair in the wrong way.'

She paused.

'It sounds crazy now, but at the time I was just so afraid of upsetting him. His moods were terrible. We were so good together when he was happy, and I wanted to do what I could to keep him that way. But I refused to cut my hair, so he told me to wear it up, so that it looked a bit less feminine. Less pretty. He began questioning me if I was ever late coming home from work. Who had I been talking to? Was it a man? Didn't I know how scared it made him feel when I didn't come home on time? It was just a part time job at a bar, to help with college fees, but he figured the place was filled with nothing but lecherous guys.'

She paused again.

'I began to realise I had no life outside of college and work. I hadn't seen my family in ages. My friends no longer asked me out. All I did was spend time in the flat with Mike. I was just eighteen. It seemed like no life at all, and I didn't want it to stay that way. It had seemed like a compliment at first, the way he seemed to need me. But I began to see that my life had become a prison. A prison I needed to escape.'

'And he let you go?'

'I waited until he went to work, then packed what few possessions I had and took a bus home to Mum. He went crazy when he came home and found out I wasn't there. Called me on my phone. When I told him we were over there was the longest silence, and then he called me all these vile names, said my life wouldn't be worth living without him, and that if I didn't come back to him by the morning I would regret it.'

'Freya…'

'I thought it was just him letting off steam. I thought he was saying stuff like that because his pride had been hurt. But he really was that crazy. I was shopping when it happened. Out on the high street and suddenly he was there, throwing acid into my face.'

'My God! I'm so sorry.'

'I should have seen it coming. I knew he couldn't let go—knew he was a little unstable. I should have expected it.'

'You can't blame yourself.'

'I do, though. For getting involved with a man like that in the first place.'

'You were just *eighteen*, Freya.'

'I know, but…but I feel I should have had more sense.'

Rebel had been up ahead, but now he came loping back, his large paws pounding the ground. He came running up to Jamie, sniffing around his jacket.

Jamie tried not to freeze. Tried to keep walking. To act normal.

'Rebel, heel!'

The dog left him instantly and went back to its mistress. Jamie breathed a sigh of relief. He understood how hard it was for Freya. She couldn't know. Even if she suspected the worst, she couldn't know if or when it would happen. It was impossible. His own hesitation and fear around dogs was similar, but Freya's fear had to be tenfold. He would do whatever he could to make things easier for her.

'You did what you thought was right at the time, with the knowledge you had. You couldn't have asked any more of yourself back then. Or now, come to think of it.'

'What are we going to do, Jamie? I can't marry you. I can't be your wife and leave everything to go and be Queen in some foreign country. That's not me. That's not what I want from my life. And I can't have my children raised behind walls with security guards for protection. I want them to be free.'

'I know. I understand. I *do*. But I can't leave you behind. A king has to be, above all, a good role model for his citizens. I can't leave my children here and go back to rule as an absent father. But I can't let my people down, either. They'll need me. At some point they'll need me on that throne.'

'We have a stalemate, then.' She pulled a small treat from her pocket and fed it to the dog.

'In the future, yes, but right now we can try and work something out.'

'How do you mean?'

'I might not have to be King for many years. In the meantime let me be with you—and them. Let me be who I need to be. I *have* to be in their lives.'

Could she hear the desperation in his voice?

She looked up at him, considering him, judging him. He knew she was still scared. There was no way that was just going to disappear. But he could see that she was thinking about acquiescing to his request.

'I want my children to know their father,' she said.

'That's good.'

'But I don't want their father running out on them. I won't have their hearts broken, Jamie. I won't.'

'I would never want to hurt them in any way.'

'But it will happen. Eventually. Wouldn't it be easier if—?'

'No.'

He knew what she was going to say. *Wouldn't it be easier for them if they just didn't know about you at all?*

'I can't forget about them. They're here. They're a part of me. They are my sons or my daughters. I can't walk away from that. Could you?'

She let out a heavy sigh. 'No, I couldn't.'

They walked on a little more. An older couple were walking towards them, holding hands, chatting. They looked so comfortable with each other. So safe in their little bubble.

He envied them. Envied them their easy lives.

'I have a responsibility to do the right thing. A father stands by his children *and* the mother of those children. As a man, I have to show them that's what I should do. Take responsibility for my actions. As King, I need to think about my people and how they need a good, strong leader they can respect. But most of all I have to respect myself, and that means doing the best by all of you. That doesn't mean, and nor would it ever mean, walking away.'

Freya nodded. 'Okay. We'll work something out.'

He nodded too, sure they would find a way.

'We will.'

'I've brought you something.' Back at work, Freya stood awkwardly in front of Jamie, holding two mugs of tea.

Jamie put down the magazine he'd been reading and looked up at her in surprise.

'It's tea.' She thrust the mug towards him.

He took it. 'Thank you. That's very kind.'

'It's just tea.'

But they both knew it was more than that. It was an olive branch. A step forward. A slight lowering of the barricades. The walls were still there. Freya didn't know if she would ever be able to trust another man. But she was willing to give him a chance to show her that she was wrong after the way he had approached Rebel. Willing to trust. Being scared, but doing it anyway.

'May I sit with you for a moment?'

'Please do.' He sat up, straightening, and watched her as she lowered herself into the chair opposite him.

'We…er…ought to get to know one another a bit more.'

He smiled, pleased. 'That's a very good idea.'

'Thank you.'

'How do you suppose we do that?'

She wasn't sure. She hadn't thought that far ahead. To be honest, she hadn't thought she'd get past offering him the tea before chickening out and walking away again, but she had done it. And now here she was.

'We should meet outside of work. What sort of things do you like to do?' he asked. 'That don't involve big dogs?'

She smiled. 'I like to read.' Then she realised that they were hardly going to sit and *read* together, were they? 'I don't really have any other hobbies.'

'What did you do when you were little? There must have been something.'

She thought for a moment. 'I loved to swim. But I haven't done that for years.'

'Swimming's very good for pregnant women. We should do that.'

'Oh, I couldn't possibly—'

'I'll arrange for us to have the pool area at my hotel all to ourselves. What day do you fancy?'

Oh. She hadn't thought he would be able to do that. But what did she know? He was a prince—he could probably do anything he wanted. He was right. There was so much they didn't know about each other. But swimming? Wearing just a swimsuit? Was it too late to back out?

'Saturday evening?' she said.

'Perfect. Thank you, Freya.'

'For what?'

'The olive branch.' He sipped at his tea and smiled. 'It tastes lovely.'

She'd had to get herself a new swimsuit, and had bought one online. She'd had to go for one especially for pregnant women, that allowed for a burgeoning belly, and had found a nice dark navy one with a crimson and cream pleat around her boobs.

Trying it on at home, she stood in front of the mirror to see what Jamie would see. She needed to shave her legs, that was for sure. Maybe paint her toenails?

The swimsuit covered her nicely, though, and even coped with her growing breasts without making her look as if she was hanging out of it. So all in all she was quite pleased with her purchase.

It revealed the scars on her neck, though.

She reached to touch the roughened skin where a graft had failed to take and was reminded of the first time she had looked in a mirror after the attack. The doctors had given her a small hand mirror and then left her to look by herself. Even her mum had left the room, giving her privacy for such a moment.

She'd almost not looked. Why had they all left like that? she'd wondered. Was it because the damage was so bad that they didn't want to see her distress?

Lifting up the mirror, turning to see, had been the most heartbreaking moment of her life. Her face had been ravaged by the acid, her nose almost gone. Angry, red, livid skin…

She'd wanted to die. Right at that moment she had thought that life was no longer worth living. That she would never look better than she did there and then. That her life was over at eighteen years of age and that she would now be one of those relatives kept hidden away in a house, never to be seen again.

But time was a great healer. And the body had an amazing ability to repair itself. It had been a long, hard, painful road, but after each surgery, after each debriding, after each skin graft, she had looked into the mirror and seen progress. Incremental progress. The skin had become less angry. Smoother. Flatter. Her nose had been re-built, new eyebrows tattooed into place.

Slowly but surely, normality had seemed to be within reach. She knew she would never be perfect again. Never have the face she used to have. But she would no longer look like some kind of monster.

She'd grown used to the scars, but to everyone she met they were brand-new and she still feared their judgement.

Swimming, though… She hadn't done it in years, because she'd been too afraid to go to a public pool. All those people? Not likely. But she had missed it. So much so, she actually felt a small frisson of excitement at the idea of having a pool to herself and just being allowed to float in the water, quiet and serene, without the worry of people watching her.

She knew she shouldn't be so sensitive to that, but she couldn't help it. A person's face was what they presented to the world, and *her* face was different. Not different in that she had too big a nose, or a massive spot on her chin. Her face just had *that look* after all the skin grafts. The hint of something that was awful underneath in the way her top lip was slightly pulled to one side, her nostrils not quite normal.

The thought of returning to the Franklin Hotel caused butterflies in her stomach. The last time she'd been there it had been made clear to her just exactly who Jamie was. This time she already knew. But he would find out who *she* was. And she wasn't used to people probing around inside her life like that.

Suck it up. You're doing this for your babies.

She parked the car and crunched across the stones on the driveway into the entrance hall. Jamie was already there, waiting to meet her, and he surprised her by kissing her on both cheeks.

'I'm glad you came.'

She nodded, trying to make sense—quickly— of how it had felt when his lips had pressed against her face. She'd stopped breathing. Felt hot. Uncertain.

It's nothing. Just get on with it.

But she hadn't been ready for him to touch her face like that. And with his lips. His perfect lips...

'Shall we go through to the pool? I can show you where the changing rooms are.'

Freya nodded hurriedly, glad that she didn't blush any more the way she'd used to. Following him through the reception area, down a small corridor, through a set of double doors, she was suddenly hit by the smell of chlorine.

It was like going back through time. She'd both forgotten that smell and remembered it intently at the same time. It was so strong! And there was that slight echo in the room, the reflection of the blue water, bouncing off the walls...

'The ladies' changing rooms are off to the right.'

'Thank you.'

Freya headed off to get changed, letting out a strained breath as she got to the changing area.

What was she doing—coming here? Doing this? Was she really about to strip down to a swimming costume in front of Jamie? It was practically like being naked. Naked meant vulnerable, and she didn't like feeling that way.

She sat down on a wooden bench for a moment, to breathe and gather herself.

I'm not doing this for me. I'm doing this for my children, so that when they're grown up I can tell them that I tried my best.

Suitably emboldened, she got up and began to undress. She put on her swimsuit and wrapped herself in a large towel before heading out to the pool.

Jamie was waiting for her. Wearing just a pair of trunks that emphasised his physique. She tried not to stare as she took in his beautiful body. His slightly hairy chest, his toned muscles, his flat stomach and long, strong, powerful thighs…

He was a thing of beauty, with his dark toned skin, whereas *she* hadn't been out in the sun for ages and was milky white, pale, swollen and…

She almost chickened out. Almost turned around to go back inside the changing room saying *I'm not doing this*, but then he smiled at her, padding towards her to take her hand.

'Are you all right?'

She nodded, not trusting herself to speak, fighting the urge to flee, but also wanting to get into that water so very much! She'd missed it. Swimming. Relaxing. Floating in the water with the weight of the world off her body.

'Let's get you in, then.'

He walked ahead of her down the steps, her hand in his, allowing her to slip off the towel and get chest-deep in the water before he turned back to look at her.

She appreciated him being a gentleman like that.

'How does the water feel?' he asked.

It felt wonderful. She felt instantly lighter— her bump supported, the strain off her back— and the temperature was perfect.

'Amazing!' She smiled, treading water and moving her arms.

'How many years has it been?'

'Erm… About twenty years. Maybe more.'

He swam alongside her, dipping his head to get his hair wet.

She glanced at him when he came up for air, and then looked away again. God, the man was sexy, all wet like that! Flustered, she allowed the weight of her legs to drop to the bottom of the pool and stood up. She was feeling strange things happening in her body. Tingling anticipation.

'When did *you* last swim?' she asked, to try and think of anything else but her body's primal reaction to this man beside her.

'Yesterday.' He smiled. 'I always do a few lengths after a shift.'

'*After?* How do you have the energy?'

'I just do. But, then again, I'm not growing babies inside me. How are you feeling?'

'Better now the morning sickness has disappeared. It wasn't too bad. I was never actually sick. But I'm feeling much better, thank you.'

'I'm glad.'

She stared at him for a moment. They were facing each other, about a metre apart, treading water. He looked so relaxed, and she wondered how he could be that way with so many worries upon his broad shoulders.

'How do you do it?'

He frowned. 'Do what?'

'Have those men following you around all the time? Your security? I've noticed I've got some of my own now. They're discreet, but they're there. It scared the hell out of me when I realised I was being followed.'

'I should have mentioned them to you. I'm sorry, I should have thought.'

'You should.'

'You get used to it. After a while you hardly notice.'

'Really?'

'Really.'

'I wonder what they think of all this? Having to follow *me* around?'

'I don't know. They do it because I order them to.'

'To protect me?'

He nodded.

'I don't need protection.'

'Maybe not, but those babies of mine do.' *Duty.* Would it always come back to that? He had a duty to his children, not to her. He *had* to do it, not because he wanted to.

She felt some similarity in her own life. She'd survived because she'd had to. She was trying to let him in because she had to. She owed it to her babies. But was it what she wanted? Yes—in a way. Her desire to be a mother was incredibly strong, and the need for her children to know their father was equally so. Even if she did suspect that at some point he would have to leave them behind.

She thought of women who were married to soldiers. Didn't they do the same thing? Knowing that at some point they might lose their husbands? That one day they just wouldn't come home?

But Jamie wouldn't be dying, would he? He would be choosing his duty, his country, over them.

She turned and began to swim breaststroke across the pool. Jamie swam alongside her. And now that the olive branch had been accepted, now that she wasn't having that knee-jerk reaction to keeping him at arm's length, she was curious about the man whose babies she was carrying. His life. His past.

'Tell me about your childhood. What was it like, growing up as a prince?'

He gave a wry smile. 'It was privileged life—no surprise there. But it was also very difficult.'

'In what way?'

'I was a young boy who wanted to run off and explore. Beyond the palace was a thriving town, and beyond that an oasis. I wanted to go there all on my own, but that was never allowed. I felt my freedom was restricted, and along with my schooling I was given many hours of instruction on politics and court etiquette and council procedures, which was all very dry and uninteresting to a boy who only wanted to be able to go to the falconry or the stables or have friends round after school.'

She tried to imagine him. Tried to imagine her own children having such a life. It didn't sound the best.

'Sounds lonely.'

'I was never lonely—which was half the trouble. There was always someone there, standing in the background, waiting, watching. Once my father had forbidden me to learn midwifery I was very angry for a while, and I would often try my best to evade my guards so I could sneak out of the palace grounds and be free for a little while.'

'Did you manage to do that often?'

He smiled. 'I did—much to their disappointment and anger. But I really felt like I didn't belong there.'

Neither did she belong there. Or her babies. It was part of their heritage, but did they deserve to spend their lives like that? Yearning for freedom and escape? She knew how that felt. She'd been there. Wanting to escape from four walls and having family and doctors constantly watching over her. It had been stifling.

'But you have a wonderful brother?'

'I do. He's only a few years older than me, so hopefully he'll be on the throne for a long time. Who knows? Maybe our children will be fully grown and living lives of their own before I have to return to Majidar.'

She stopped swimming as she came to the edge of the pool and leaned back against it. Wouldn't it be wonderful if it happened that way?

'I hope so, Jamie. I do.'

He smiled, before sinking under the surface and swimming towards her, rising from the depths like a merman, his face right in front of hers. It was unnerving, having him this close. She could see him looking at her, taking in every feature of her face.

'Tell me about *your* childhood, Freya.'

His dark eyes were looking into her own with such concentration. Nervous, she began to talk.

'I've lived my whole life here in Chichester. I was very much a girly girl, playing with dolls and babies. I would line them all up like they were in a hospital nursery, covered with little blankets I'd made myself on my mother's sewing machine.'

'You can sew?'

She shrugged. 'Moderately. Simple things— cushions, blankets, curtains.'

'Go on.'

'I loved to play mum. I wanted a brother or sister desperately, but I never got one.'

It had been lonely, growing up without siblings. At least her twins would have each other. Didn't twins usually have a strong bond?

'I loved to swim. I wanted to have horse-riding lessons, but Mum could never afford it.'

'I have horses.'

She lifted her eyebrows in surprise, smiling. 'You do?'

'In Majidar, yes.'

'Oh.'

'Beautiful stallions. Racehorses.'

'Do you miss them?'

'I'm kept up to date on their progress.'

'But only from afar. It must be hard to be kept from something you love?'

Jamie stared at her. 'It can be.'

She could see him having a proper look now. Seeing the edges of her scars around her hairline. Tracking the damage that must have been done and had been repaired. Realising how many operations she must have gone through to look as she did today.

The intense scrutiny made her uncomfortable.

'Love does strange things to people. Makes them act out of character. Makes them crazy. Makes them not think straight.'

Jamie's hand reached up out of the water and

she sucked in a breath as his fingers traced the edges of her face, down her cheek, along her jaw. Such a tender touch—respectful and gentle.

'You're beautiful, you know?'

What?

She hadn't expected him to say that. Never in a million years had she expected to hear *anyone* say that to her. Not the way he had. As if he meant it. He'd not been patronising her. His voice had spoken the truth as he saw it.

Moved to strong emotion, Freya blinked back tears at his words.

'Have I upset you?'

'No.' She wiped her eyes hurriedly and tried to smile bravely, to show him that she was okay. Her mum would tell her she was beautiful, but she'd always dismissed that—mums were duty-bound to say that.

'You're crying.' He reached out and pulled her gently towards him.

At first she resisted. Just slightly. But then she gave in, allowing herself that moment. She rested her head against his shoulder, put her arms around his back, completely in shock that this was even happening. This, she had *not* expected. To be held like this…

'I'm okay,' she said, her face against his wet shoulder.

His hand smoothed down her hair. 'No, you're not. But I'll hold you until you are.'

And he did. They both stood there, in the warmth of the pool, in each other's arms, until the tears dried in her eyes, she stopped sniffing and the water was still, like a pond.

When everything was calm again, and her breathing had settled into a steady in and out motion, she felt him release her.

'We should have a change of scene. Let's go to dinner,' he said. 'Before you get cold.'

And she suddenly couldn't think of anything she wanted more than to sit with him. Talk. This man had been nothing but gentlemanly and kind to her. He'd never shown her pity. Never reacted the way everyone else had.

'I'd love to have dinner with you.' She meant it. Smiled her thanks. And, though she tried her hardest not to look down at his mouth, at those lips that had once brushed her skin in the most intimate way, she couldn't help herself.

She wondered what it would be like to let down her guard completely and kiss him all over again?

The hotel's restaurant was dimly lit, and they were seated in a small alcove near the back, away from prying eyes, where they could pretend it was just the two of them.

From the reception area she could hear the piano being played—gentle, soothing music.

She'd got out of the pool and gone back to the changing room to get dressed on very shaky legs, unsure as to what was happening between the two of them. She wanted to let him in—but just a little bit. To let him know that they could talk about things, discuss the future. But something else seemed to have happened. An anticipation of so much more.

Hope.

Never in her wildest dreams had she ever thought she would be in this position—pregnant, about to become a mother, but also having a man tell her that she was *beautiful*.

It was a word she'd never thought would be used to describe her again. *Brave* got used an awful lot. *Courageous. Stubborn*, maybe.

But beautiful?

She'd stared at the mirror as she blow-dried her hair, focusing intently on her own face, gazing at the façade that it had taken her years to get used to. Inside, she still felt that she looked the way she had before the accident, so every time she looked in the mirror it was a stark reminder that she was different.

She'd tried to embrace that and look forward. Never allowing the melancholy and disappointment to overwhelm her. Never letting what Mike had done beat her down, because then he would have done what he'd set out to do. Never allowing the depression to set in, as it had with so many others affected in a similar way.

She was living the best way that she could. Under *her* rules. *Her* control. And now she was handing some of that control over to him.

She was different now. Not just in looks, but in character. She cared more for the underdogs in society; she listened, empathised, and she worked damned hard to make sure her patients felt empowered and brave and strong. She was their cheerleader. Their support. She knew she could coach women through the scariest moments of their lives, even as they felt they were being split in two, and she knew they *all* had the strength within them to get through it. She gave them everything they needed and asked for nothing in return.

But now Jamie was here and he wanted to pay her attention. He wasn't family, but he was trying to give her everything she needed and a whole lot more besides. He was able, it seemed, to see past the prickly exterior that she had first presented to him. He had pushed it to one side, had powered through, because he was invested in *her* well-being. *Her* thoughts and feelings. *Her* health. *Her* happiness.

And that felt odd. Disconcerting.

Good, but strange.

It had happened at university, too. During her training. Her teachers and lecturers had seen past her face and made sure she qualified, made sure she became the midwife she'd always wanted to be.

Perhaps she needed to give more people the benefit of the doubt?

'I'll have the Caesar salad to start, please, and I think I'll have the pan-seared chicken for my main, thank you,' she said to the waiter from behind her menu card.

'Smoked salmon and the pheasant for me, thanks.'

The waiter disappeared, having removed the menu cards with him.

Freya took a sip of her water. 'You must be used to English food now. Is there anything you miss from back home that you can't get here?'

'You don't serve as much goat as there was back home.' He smiled. 'Or *luqmat al-qadi*.'

She frowned, having never heard of that before. 'What is that?'

'They're like your pastries. A leavened dough that has been deep-fried, then soaked in a very sweet syrup.'

'Like a doughnut?'

'Not quite. My mother made them. Sometimes

she would add cinnamon or sweet spices to them. They were out of this world.'

'Your mother cooked?'

'Occasionally. Not as often as she would have liked.'

'My mum likes to cook. She likes to feed people. There's always something on at her house.'

'It was the same at mine.'

She smiled. 'But, to be fair, your house was a palace, so...'

He laughed, good-naturedly. 'True.'

She took another sip of water. 'Is your mother still alive?'

His eyes darkened. 'No. She passed away a few months after my father did. It was a huge shock to lose them both so quickly like that. But I believe she died of a broken heart, after losing my father so suddenly.'

'She must have loved him very much.'

He nodded. 'Al Bakharis love deeply.'

Her breath caught in her throat as she imagined that sort of passion. The depth of love that one person could have for another. It was the type of love she had once imagined for herself. The type of love she had thought she had found with Mike, in the way he had so quickly and deeply fallen for her.

That kind of love was scary. Terrifying. It could totally condemn you to a future filled with pain, misery and grief. Case in point: Jamie's mother dying of a broken heart. Perhaps love was more dangerous than people realised and they were fools to seek it out? It was best to keep things light. Casual. Even if it did leave you wanting…

'Have you ever felt that way about someone?' she asked.

'Not yet. That kind of love is the kind that stays for eternity. You will always be together, until the end of your days. If I had already found that, then you and I would not be in the situation we now find ourselves in.'

It was a stark reminder of exactly what this was between them.

A *situation*.

That was all. There was no point in reading anything else into it—even if he *had* told her she was beautiful. Even though he had cradled her in his arms until she'd stopped crying. Even if they had shared that one magical night together.

They'd been caught out by Mother Nature and now they were having to deal with the consequences.

That was all this was. Nothing more, nothing less.

So, despite the fact that they were sitting together in a restaurant, having only just a few minutes before shared a most intimate connection as she was wrapped in his embrace, Freya had to remind herself not to get carried away with *hope*. With *possibility*.

But she'd always been a dreamer and it was hard to switch that part of her brain off.

If the accident hadn't happened she would never have been at that charity ball. She would never have had that night with Jamie. She wouldn't be pregnant with twins. But they still would have met at work, and she would still have been attracted to him. The way she was now.

It was hard to tell herself that he probably didn't feel the same way. No matter what he'd said.

Reality hurt when she thought about that. She might have defied the odds and got pregnant, but Jamie was *not* going to be her knight in shining armour and she would do well to remember that.

'Please excuse me a moment.'

She stood, needing to escape to the bathroom for a minute alone—because she could feel tears threatening to fall down her face, and if she cried again he would comfort her again. He would touch her. Hold her. Try to make her feel better. And, despite her best instincts, she realised she *wanted* that.

Even though she shouldn't.

And she couldn't have that.

She stared at her tear-stained reflection in the bathroom mirror.

Why was life testing her so harshly?

CHAPTER FIVE

JAMIE WAS VERY pleased with the way their relationship was progressing. Freya's walls were starting to come down, and now she was letting him sit and talk to her at work. They socialised together sometimes, getting to know one another, and when they went to her check-ups and other appointments with her consultant they asked questions as if they were a real couple.

He'd sat by her side when she'd had her twenty-one-week scan, gripping her hand tightly in his, and they'd both been over the moon when the scan had confirmed that they were going to have non-identical twin boys.

Sons!

That was a big deal for Jamie. He'd always dreamed of having sons and raising them to be good, strong men. Sons to be proud of…sons he would support in their desire to do anything. He would not restrict their lives the way his had been, and if they wanted to become pilots or nurses, whatever their dreams could possibly be, he vowed to himself that he would help them achieve them in any way that he could.

His sons would be his heirs. Heirs to the throne. It was their destiny, but what would they know of it? What would they know of Majidar? With its rolling dunes, its intense heat and its beautiful people. He himself had yearned to leave and live a life he couldn't get there. Should he be the one to tell them that they must follow that path when he didn't want it for himself? Who was he to decide what they should do? He was their father, so shouldn't he want them to be happy more than anything else?

He'd sent news of the babies to his brother Ilias and younger sister Zahra. Both had responded with joy and delight, but both had asked him when he was coming home. With Freya at his side.

It was an awkward question to which he had no answer.

Zahra was already gushing about their wedding and all the things they'd need to organise. How could he tell her that it was probably never going to happen?

So he'd kept silent, swearing them to secrecy in his last email, until he knew what the next few months would bring. He'd used work as his main excuse. Said he was still under contract

for another six months, with the possibility of a
permanent post, and that he would not let people down when they were depending upon him.

Zahra had emailed back.

Six months? But the babies will be born by then!

It was all so difficult. So confusing. If he'd
had his way then he and Freya would already
be married. No need for a big ceremony in Majidar...no need to be driven down the streets in
an open-topped car, waving to adoring crowds.
He would present his marriage as a *fait accom-
pli*. Everyone would just have to accept it.

If only Freya would accept it!

That would be easier, wouldn't it?

He hadn't mentioned it to her for a while, not
wanting to raise such a difficult subject again
when things between them seemed to be going
so well.

When he'd first mentioned marriage he'd done
it out of duty. Done it because of the moral code
that told him it was the right thing to do. Not for
him, or for her, but for their children. Whether
Freya liked it or not, her babies carried royal
blood and he would not have them being illegitimate. He hadn't thought too much about whether
a marriage between them would work out or not.
It just had to be. Details, emotions, feelings—all

those could be worked out later, as time allowed them to know each other more.

But now…?

Life was even more complicated.

He liked Freya a lot. He cared for her. And the more he got to know her, the more he realised that if they were to get married then he would have a happy life with her, a happy marriage. He felt it in his bones. She was strong and loving and kind, the bravest woman he had ever known, and he felt proud that a woman like that was carrying his children. What a role model she would be! How much she would love them!

His feelings for her were deepening every day. Each time she laughed or smiled his heart expanded a little bit more. Each time she trusted him with a hint of intimacy—a confession, a secret, a story from her past—his feelings for her grew.

It was confusing. The line between emotion and duty was blending, merging. How could he get her to understand how he felt if he didn't even understand it, himself?

It was the end of November, and at seven months pregnant Freya felt huge. It had been many weeks since she had last been able to reach her own feet, and she thanked the Lord that Jamie, at least, seemed quite happy to lift her feet up onto his lap and massage them for her when they had a break at work.

Her body was protesting. She was knocking back strawberry milkshakes as if they were going out of fashion, and she dreaded to think about how much extra weight she was putting on. But it was all for a good cause, so she was trying to be relaxed about it.

There wasn't long left, and this probably wouldn't happen again, so she was trying to enjoy her pregnancy for as long as she could.

The babies were good movers, kicking and stretching at all hours of the day and night, and she would often sit at work with one hand on her swollen baby, feeling their movements. It was very reassuring.

They were good sizes, too. She and Jamie had attended many scans which had not only marked the growth of the babies, but also the growth of their ever-changing relationship.

She'd started to get the nursery ready at home. Jamie had even come over one evening to help paint the walls and put up some stencils. He'd even climbed a ladder to hang up the new curtains she'd made.

It was almost as if they were a real couple getting ready for their future.

Only without the living together and the sex.

And sex had been high on her mind lately, despite her burgeoning size. It had to be the hormones! She was blaming them entirely as her mind filled with X-rated images of her and Jamie doing really naughty things together.

It didn't help that he was so easy on the eye. Or that he was kind and thoughtful and gentlemanly. Seeing him smile delighted her, and she often found herself reaching out to touch him—a hand on his arm, his shoulder. Touching the small of his back as she passed behind him at work. Just a small contact. But enough to make her desires surge and make her brain remind her of what that one night had been like and how wonderful it would feel to experience that again. To touch him in other places. To have him touch her...

Enough, Freya!

It would never be like that between them again.

Would it?

She blinked, trying to dismiss the thrilling images she'd created, and instead focused on the patient notes she was filling out. Her patient, Rosie Clay, had been progressing through labour quite well until suddenly the baby had started showing decelerations. The infant had gone into distress and Rosie had been rushed to theatre for an emergency Caesarean section. Rosie was now fine, but her baby girl was in the NICU, having aspirated meconium, which meant she had passed her first stool whilst still in the womb.

She dropped the pen to stretch out her shoulders, thrusting them back and trying to roll them. She suddenly felt hands slide down over them.

'Tense?' Jamie asked.

You betcha.

'Yeah, a little. It got a bit frantic in Theatre just now.'

'I heard. The baby's in NICU?'

'A little girl.'

'Little girls are strong.'

She thought of her own babies. Of the struggles they might have in the future together. Alone, without a father.

'So are little boys.'

Jamie's hands felt great, massaging away the tenseness of her muscles, releasing the knots and strain that she'd been carrying all night. She could groan because he was making her feel so good!

'You can stop now.'

She pulled away, not wanting to embarrass herself. Jamie was just doing it out of duty, anyway. She'd accepted that ages ago, and reminded herself daily not to get too carried away with what was happening between them. It was the babies he was interested in. And she was dreaming again. Allowing herself to get carried away with fantasy.

It was her ability to dream and fantasise that had got her through the long, painful days after her attack; it had been the only way she could escape the pain and the four walls that had bound her so tightly.

He settled into a seat beside her. 'Do you need anything to drink? Eat?'

'No, I'm fine, thank you,' she answered, and heard a harshness coming out in her voice that she hadn't intended. But this was so frustrating! Having something so close she could almost touch it. Wanting something—*someone*—so badly, but knowing it could never happen.

'You're sure?'

She nodded, fighting the urge to yell at him, to tell him to leave her alone because that was what he was going to do anyway. At some point. And the idea of it was breaking her heart.

She'd grown to love his friendship, his kindness, his support—even his attentiveness. But sometimes she got angry—mostly with herself—knowing it wouldn't be for ever.

Freya had tried to keep herself distanced from it, but lately it had become nigh on impossible and her hormones were probably to blame for that too! It was as if her body had become conditioned to let him in. To allow him to care for her as the natural father of her children. But she had other feelings developing too, and they were dangerous and stupid!

Beside them, the buzzer rang. Someone required admission.

In the evening, the doors were locked for security, so anyone turning up in the middle of the night, in labour or otherwise, had to buzz to be let in. There was a security camera so the staff could see who was there.

Freya looked at the monitor and its grainy black and white image. A man stood there, desperately looking up at the camera, wrapped in a coat and scarf.

She picked up the phone to speak through the intercom. 'Hello?'

'My wife! My wife's having the baby!'

'Okay, sir, I'm going to buzz you through.' She went to press the button.

'No, you don't understand! She's having it *now*. In the car! I can see the head!'

Freya glanced at Jamie, who got up at a run and raced down the corridor, grabbing a mobile pack from the supply room as he did so.

'Someone will be with you in a moment. Hang on!'

She knew she wouldn't be able to run like Jamie, but he would need back-up. It was freezing out. And there was a frost.

She got to her feet and moved down the corridor as fast as she could, her feet protesting, the babies kicking at the sudden rush of adrenaline in her system. She grabbed extra blankets and slapped the button release to open the doors, then took the stairs.

It would be quicker than waiting for the lift. It was just two flights.

She held her belly with one hand as she hurried down the stairs, her other hand on the rail, and by the time she got to the bottom she was out of breath and the twins were kicking madly. She burst through another set of double doors, hurried across the lobby and pressed the buzzer for the outer doors, feeling a wall of cold air hit her as she raced outside.

There was a car parked in the dropping-off bay, its doors open on one side—the guy from the monitor was in the front and Jamie was crouching by the back. She could see there was already a little bit of ice forming on the path. She hoped the gritters would be along soon…

'That's it, Catherine, push as hard as you can!' she heard Jamie say.

'What have we got?' She pulled her penlight torch from her top pocket and shone it into the interior of the car.

A woman was lying in the back, her dress up around her waist and her baby's head already born. There was no point in trying to get this patient into a wheelchair and whizzed upstairs now. She was going to have this baby in the car.

'Catherine—thirty-nine, forty weeks' gestation.'

'Okay, anything we need to be worried about?'

'Just the cold.'

'I've brought extra blankets.'

Jamie turned to grab them and laid them over the headrest, so they'd be ready when he needed them. He already had his gloves on, had the kit open, and was ready to clip off the cord.

'Catherine, one more push with the next contraction. I want you to push as hard as you can, okay? Let's get this baby out and safe into your arms.'

Catherine nodded furiously, sucked in a huge breath and began to push.

At first nothing happened, and for a brief second Freya worried about there being a possible shoulder dystocia, but then slowly the baby began to emerge. Catherine sucked in another breath and began to push again, and this time the baby slithered out, crying immediately in protest.

'Well done, Catherine!' Jamie had caught the baby and immediately put it into its mother's arms, grabbing the blankets to drape over them both before he clipped and cut the cord.

'Oh, my God!' Catherine cried, looking down at her baby with love and joy.

'You did it! You gave birth in the car!' cried the new dad. 'The upholstery's probably ruined, but I don't care!'

Behind her, Freya heard the doors open and Mona appeared, pushing a wheelchair. They needed to get the new mum and baby inside so they could do the proper checks and get the placenta delivered.

Jamie took the baby and passed it to Freya, so that he could help get Catherine out of the car, lowering her gently into the wheelchair. She was shivering and shaking, so he wrapped the last blanket around her shoulders.

'Let's get her inside.'

They all hurried into the lobby, and Freya pressed the button for the lift before passing the baby back to its mother.

Catherine gazed into the loving eyes of her husband. 'We have a *son*!'

The man laid his forehead against his wife's and kissed her. 'We do. Well done! I'm so proud of you.'

He turned to look at Freya and Jamie.

'I'm Martin—pleased to meet you.' He shook their hands. 'This little one is so precious to us. He's an IVF baby.'

'Congratulations.'

'We thought we'd left it too late, but now we have him. A son. Thank you all so much!'

'Catherine did all the hard work,' said Freya, and smiled.

The lift doors pinged open and they wheeled Catherine through to an empty room and helped her onto the bed. They injected the syntocinon and the placenta was delivered almost without Catherine noticing as she cradled her little boy.

'Have you thought of a name yet?' asked Freya, who'd donned gloves and was beginning to check it.

Catherine smiled wanly, looking tired. 'Jackson.'

'That's a beautiful name.'

But something was wrong. The placenta was not as it should be. Freya felt the hairs go up on the back of her neck and instinctively knew. Catherine had gone incredibly pale, and now she rested her head back against the pillow.

She caught the baby before Catherine could drop him. 'Martin, take the baby!'

'What's going on?'

Jamie lifted up the sheet and grimaced. 'Haemorrhage.'

He smacked the red button behind Catherine's head and an alarm sounded. Before they knew it the room was filling with people and Catherine was being whisked out on her bed, headed for Theatre. Jamie went with them.

Freya was left with Martin and the baby, in a room with blood all over the floor.

'What just happened?' asked Martin.

'It looks like Catherine is losing too much blood.' She examined the placenta more and realised there was a piece missing. 'Retained placenta. That's why she began to bleed so heavily.' She laid a hand upon his arm. 'They'll look after her.'

'I *can't* lose her. I can't lose my wife!'

'Come and take a seat, Martin.'

She guided him safely to a chair and helped him sit. She needed to examine the baby, but she was very conscious of the fact that Martin would probably be reluctant to hand his son over right now.

'Emergencies can be frightening, but she was in the right place when it happened. If she'd given birth earlier and you hadn't made it here... You did, though. She's in good hands.'

'She'll be okay?'

'Everyone will do their best.'

She couldn't promise him anything. She couldn't tell him everything would be all right because she didn't know. Haemorrhages happened, and sometimes they went badly. The medical team would do everything they could for her.

'I need to check Jackson. I'll just take him over

to this cot—is that okay? You can come with me. Watch what I'm doing.'

He nodded and handed her the baby.

Freya took him gently and with the utmost respect. This man had just watched his wife collapse and be taken from him. He felt lost and bereft, and the only thing he had to cling on to with any certainty was his son.

She decided to talk him through it, so he would understand all that she was doing. If he understood what she was doing perhaps he would feel he had a bit of control over *something*.

'First I'll check his breathing.' She looked to Martin to make sure he was listening.

He nodded.

'He cried immediately after birth, and his respiratory rate is good, so he scores two points on the APGAR scale. The scale is out of ten points overall, and the higher the score, the better.'

'Okay…'

'Now I'm going to use my stethoscope to check his heart rate, and this is the most important.'

She put the earbuds in her ears and laid the stethoscope on Jackson's chest. Over a hundred beats per minute.

'He scores two for this as well. His heart rate is *good*, Martin.'

'Good.'

'Next I need to check his muscle tone, and I can see here that he has good active motion, so again he scores two.'

She talked Martin through checking for a grimace response or reflex irritability, and because Jackson began to cry she again scored him two.

'And now skin colour. His entire body is nicely pink, except his hands and feet, but that's normal. His circulation is good, so that's another point. A score of nine. You have a healthy little baby boy, Martin.' She wrapped Jackson up again and handed him back to his father. 'Do you have clothes and a nappy for him?'

Martin thought for a moment. 'Oh, it's all in the car.'

It was important to get Jackson dressed and wrapped up warmly. 'I can go and fetch them for you, if you want?'

'Would you mind?'

'Of course not.'

He reached into his back pocket and pulled out some keys. 'It's all in the boot. The lock release is on the key fob.'

'Okay. I'll do that, and then I'll get you a cup of tea. I think you've earned it.'

'You too, I would imagine.' He looked at her belly. 'How far along are you?'

'Seven months. With twins.'

'Life's about to get crazy for us all, then?'

She nodded. He had no idea how crazy her life already was.

'I'll be back in a few minutes. Any problems, just hit the orange call button on the side of the bed. Someone will come and check on you.'

She closed the door behind her and began to waddle down the corridor once again.

Boy, were her ankles killing her! And what a night shift this was turning out to be! The last time she'd helped deliver a baby in a car parked outside it had been in the middle of summer, when the nights were a lot warmer and they didn't have to worry about tiny babies freezing in the night air.

And this had been her first delivery working with Jamie. Usually they got to work alone, sometimes with another midwife, but she'd not yet had the chance to watch him in action like that. She'd been with him in Theatre before, but that had been different—their patient had been unconscious under a general anaesthetic, because it had been an emergency delivery.

Tonight she'd seen how good he was with a patient. How calm and encouraging. How he'd coached his patient to breathe and push. She could see why he loved midwifery so much, because he'd simply been alive with all that had been going on around him, and even though it had been an unusual delivery, out of the hospital, he had remained cool and in control. Even when the haemorrhage had begun he had worked quickly and calmly.

The lift doors pinged open. She didn't feel like taking the stairs again so soon. She waddled her way across the lobby and opened the double doors to go outside. The cold air hit her again and she glanced down at the keys in her hand to see which side of the fob she needed to open the boot of the car.

She walked straight out, without thinking, onto the pathway, and it happened almost instantly.

Her feet began to slide on the black ice, she lost her footing and slipped and, not having any control over her centre of gravity, she went up into the air backwards, her arms flailing, and landed heavily on the ground, the back of her head smacking hard onto the concrete.

Pain shot through her skull and her back and her belly. She reached up to rub at her head, but felt the world begin to fade and grow dark.

The last thing she saw was the clear dark sky, inky black with shining stars twinkling way beyond her, and then there was the sight of two men in dark suits appearing over her, one reaching into his jacket for a walkie-talkie and saying something in a language she didn't understand.

She closed her eyes and drifted away.

* * *

Jamie was relieved. They'd managed to save their patient. Catherine's haemorrhage had been contained, the retained piece of placenta removed and checked. The bleeding had slowed and Catherine's womb had contracted fully. Her pressure was slowly coming back up and her heart rate was getting better.

The surgeons had done it.

He let out a huge sigh of relief and removed his mask and gown, disposing of them in the trash and going to wash his hands, whilst a porter took his patient to a side room for recovery and to be monitored.

It had been touch and go there for a while, he thought as he stood washing his hands. But they had prevailed. *All* of them. Working together to save their patient and give her a chance at life. There was nothing like this feeling in the whole wide world. This miracle they called life. He watched new life coming into the world every day, and it was a privilege to be amongst those who helped women achieve it.

Days like today reiterated for him the rightness of his choice. It had been *right* to leave Majidar, and it had been *right* to pursue this dream of his. Look at what he had done this night. Earlier he'd delivered one baby, safely in a hospital bed, and now he'd safely delivered not only a baby in a car, but a mother too. Everyone in the team had done that.

Outside, he could hear a bit of a commotion. Loud voices. Men. His guards, by the sound of it. What on earth was going on?

He dried his hands on paper towels and disposed of them in the bin. He wanted to see whatever this noise was about, sort it out, and then go check on the new baby. He'd delivered the little boy—it was up to him to write up the notes.

When he pushed through the doors he froze as he saw his security men were on the ward, arguing with Jules. Whatever were they doing in here? Why did they seem so upset? They had strict instructions not to come onto the ward unless there was a just cause.

The only thing he could think of was Freya, but she'd been safe in that delivery room when he'd left with his patient for Theatre, so that left something to do with his brother the King.

Ilias? No, it can't be. He's sick, sometimes, but it can't be now!

Jules threw her hands into the air as the two guards barged past her towards Jamie.

'Jamie, these men—'

'Sadiq? Mujab? What's going on?'

But before they could say anything Jules barged through them and laid a hand upon his arm. 'It's Freya. She's had an accident.'

CHAPTER SIX

IT WAS THE pain she felt first, as she began to become aware of the world once more. Everything felt sore, but the worst thing was her headache. It was as if she had a crown of intense burning fire around her skull. Her mouth felt dry too, and she tried to lick her lips.

'Freya? Open your eyes.'

Jamie.

Jamie was here. Why was he in her bedroom? What had happened?

As she struggled to implement his instruction to open her eyes she began to remember some weird, hazy things.

A woman in a car.

A baby wrapped in blankets in her arms.

The cold.

A set of car keys.

The twinkling stars above.

Two stern-looking men crouching over her, babbling in a language she didn't understand.

And then she remembered.

The black ice.

Slipping on the pavement and falling.

She opened her eyes, struggling to focus, but she could only just make out a face. A man's face. Dark hair and midnight eyes.

'Jamie…'

She saw a relieved smile break across his face and she tried to reach up to touch him, to make sure he was real, but it was as if she was unco-ordinated, or didn't have the strength.

'You've had a nasty fall. Knocked yourself out. The babies are okay. You've had a little bleed-ing, but they're okay. We're keeping you in for monitoring and bed rest.'

Freya blinked as she processed this huge amount of information. 'What? Keeping me in? No.'

She panicked, tried to get up, tried to get out of bed, but dizziness assailed her and she felt his firm hands holding her arms, pressing her down.

'You need to stay in bed.'

'No, I'm—'

'Freya, for once you are going to have to do as you are told!'

And then she heard it in his voice. *Fear.*

He *cared.*

She blinked again and tried to focus on his

face, but she just felt so tired. Slowly, inexorably, her eyes closed once again and she drifted off to sleep.

'Concussion?' She stared at Jamie.

'Yes. You're also still bleeding and you have high blood pressure, so you're staying in on bed rest.'

Staying in. In hospital.

Adrenaline was pulsing through her, making her legs twitch. She wanted to run. Wanted to get out of there.

'But the babies are fine, you said.'

'I did.'

'But I need to stay on bed rest? Are you kidding me?'

'What would *you* say to a patient seven months pregnant with twins, who's had a nasty fall, hit her head, has high BP and is bleeding? Would you tell her to carry on, or would you tell her to stay in bed?'

She bit her bottom lip, eyeing the door. He was right, but she didn't want to admit it. She *would* tell a patient in that situation that she needed to stay in. But this was different.

She'd been trapped in a hospital bed before. Lying there, gripping onto the bedrails, whilst a doctor and a nurse debrided the dead tissue from her face. It had felt as if the acid was being splashed onto her all over again. The pain inter-minable.

Being back in a hospital bed, being told she had to stay there, was making her feel trapped. Claustrophobic. As if she couldn't breathe.

She turned away, upset but not wanting to let him see her cry, her gaze falling on the fruit bas-kets and the balloons filling her room and all the cards on the windowsill that sent best wishes from her work colleagues and her family.

It was all terribly familiar. She was unable to move, feeling terrified and afraid. Her own life was out of her control. In the hands of doctors.

How had she forgotten what that felt like?

'I'm not sure I can do this,' she whispered.

'You have to.'

'You can't make me. I can discharge myself.'

'You'd have to get past the guards I'll put on your door first.' He raised an eyebrow. Daring her to challenge his authority.

She stared at him. He'd never ordered her about like this before. Never challenged her.

She baulked at his attempt. 'You wouldn't...?'

He leaned forward over the end of the bed. 'Try me. I've let you do this your way ever since day one. I have acquiesced to your wishes and tried my best not to upset you. But, damn you, Freya, if you get out of that bed and endanger yourself and those babies then, so help me, I will not be held responsible for my actions!'

He meant it. Every word.

She crossed her arms and looked away.

Again her life was being taken out of her control by other people. She had vowed never to let that happen to her again. This was *her* life and she wanted to be the one in charge, making all the decisions.

However, she had no doubt that he would post guards on her door, and then everyone would know who Jamie was. And as soon as that little nugget got out her life would most definitely not be her own. There would be reporters and gossip and her happy, quiet little life, hidden away on the night shift, would be destroyed.

'Fine.'

It wasn't fine. Far from it. But this wasn't just about her any more. She wasn't in this bed alone. She had two babies to think of.

He stared hard at her, his hands on his hips. 'Fine?'

'I'll stay in bed.'

'Good.'

'But on one condition.'

There was that eyebrow again. Wary. 'Yes?'

'Someone brings me a goddamned strawberry milkshake!'

There was the ghost of a smile and then he bowed, almost to the floor. 'Yes, Your Majesty.'

Freya was a cranky patient. Short on temper, irritable, bad of mood. Nervous.

But didn't they say that medics made the worst patients?

'I know it's difficult, but you need to try and relax,' he'd told her.

She'd glared at him. 'How can I? When being here reminds me of what it was like before?'

He'd placed his hand on hers. 'I know. But this is different. No one is going to hurt you now. I won't let them.'

She'd had another scan, and the babies looked fine. The consultant believed the bleeding was coming from a small lesion on her cervix, but it was nothing sinister. They'd tested it and believed the lesion had occurred as a result of her fall. The pressure of two babies on her cervix as well as the severity of the impact of her hitting the concrete had caused a small tear.

He'd given her books to read, had brought delicious yet healthy treats, and he would often sit with her, slowly massaging her feet or her shoulders as she tried to relax.

His favourite moments were spent watching her as she read. The small divot that formed between her brows, the cute way she sometimes bit her bottom lip, the way she would hurriedly turn the page, as if she just couldn't wait to find out what would happen next. Those were the moments when she forgot where she was.

She looked up at him and caught him staring. 'What are you doing?'

He smiled. 'Looking at you.'

Freya frowned and smiled at the same time. 'Well, don't.'

'Why not?'

'It's weird. I don't like people looking at me.'

'No, and you don't like people making assumptions about what happened to you. You don't like people showing sympathy. Was I doing *any* of those things?'

She looked as if she was thinking about that. 'I guess not.'

'Well, then, I'll continue to look at you.'

'But why?'

'Because I like doing it.'

It was true. He did. She was such a complicated person, prickly when scared, but fascinating. And she really was beautiful. Outwardly and inside. Her scars—shocking because of how she'd got them—were totally a part of her character. Who she was.

'But why?' She really sounded confused.

He sighed. 'Does it ever occur to you that you might be worth looking at?'

Her eyes clouded over. 'No.'

'Well, then, you're wrong.'

'Are you sure *you* didn't get the bump on the head? Perhaps you should be lying here instead of me?'

'Perhaps I should be lying *next* to you? Beside you?'

That stopped her from speaking. She immediately looked down at her book, tried to read on, but he could see that she wasn't taking anything in.

Eventually she looked up at him, exasperated, and said, 'You can't say things like that, Jamie. It's not fair.'

'Even if it's true?'

'Even if it's true. Even if you did want to be lying here next to me you shouldn't say it—because then I start to get the feelings, and I don't want to get the feelings, because some day you're going to leave. You'll leave us, Jamie, you *will*. You can't deny that.'

No. He couldn't. She was right. One day he would get called back and then what? If he tried to start a relationship with this woman it would always be there, hanging over them like a swinging blade, ready to fall down and sever them in two. Was that fair? On either of them? On the babies?

'I'll go and make us some tea.'

He got up and slipped from the room, his mind dark with thoughts of ascension to the throne and responsibility and living a life behind walls. Never to enjoy himself again. Never to deliver another baby.

Away from Freya and his sons.

He fought the urge to punch a wall. It was all just so maddening! He'd fought to get access into her life, which she had finally given, and they were becoming used to one another, liked one another—but for what?

Either way, he was going to lose someone or something.

Majidar, or Freya and the babies.

Or maybe he'd just lose himself?

'Mona, please stop fussing.' Freya laid a hand on her friend's as she continued to fiddle about with Freya's sheets.

If she was going to visit, she'd prefer it if her friend just kept her up to date with what was happening on the ward, had a cup of tea with her and chatted. Not fussed about like an old mother hen.

'I can't help it.'

Freya smiled. 'Sit. Eat one of these.' She passed over a box of chocolates that her mum had brought on her last visit. 'They're truffles.'

'Oh! Okay.' Mona took the box.

'The praline one is nice.'

Mona checked to see which one that was, and then popped it into her mouth and began to make appreciative sounds.

'Told you.'

Freya lay back against the pillows and turned away from the bright light pouring in through the window. It made a pleasant change from the dark, grey wintry days they had been having recently. Life was passing her by and she was still stuck here.

'I got the Christmas decorations out just now. I'm going to pop them up later.'

Freya frowned. 'It's still November.'

'It's never too early.'

'I beg to differ.'

'Well, *you* would. You've always been a Grumpus around Christmas.'

Mona was wrong. Freya loved Christmas. But these last few years she'd begun to resent it. Everyone she knew was married or in a relationship, or had kids, or both, so they had a reason to enjoy Christmas. They were with their loved ones. They were making memories. For Freya every Christmas was spent with her mum, and though she loved her mum it wasn't what Freya wanted.

She had big dreams of what Christmas should be. Of a Christmas morning on which she could sit and watch her children open their presents with squeals of delight. Of a festive season during which she could go out and build snowmen and have snowball fights, visit Santa in his grotto, go to see a pantomime.

Her mum was great company, but she didn't want to do any of those things. She liked a quiet, understated Christmas, where her only concern was whether the turkey would be cooked and whether they'd finish eating in time to watch the Queen's Speech. Then she'd fall asleep in her chair, until Freya woke her later in the evening to see if she wanted a mince pie.

'Wait 'til next Christmas. You'll have twins!' exclaimed Mona.

Freya nodded. But would she be alone with them? Or would Jamie be there? How was she going to cope with raising two babies? She would have to brave *everything*. Living during the day time. Seeing all those people. Changing her shifts at work because the hospital nursery only took children during daylight hours.

Her whole life was going to change.

It wasn't meant to have happened like this! She was meant to have been *happy*! Thrilled that she was having children. She *was* thrilled, but it wasn't turning out to be the fairy tale she'd imagined it would be.

'Are you and Jamie spending Christmas together?'

'I think he's working.'

'But he'll have *some* time at home. Are you going to do anything special?'

'I don't think so. I'll be at Mum's, as usual, I guess.'

'You aren't spending *any* time together?'

This line of questioning was making her feel very uncomfortable. 'He hasn't said anything.'

Mona handed her back the box of chocolates, looking sceptical. 'Is there something you're not telling me, Freya?'

'Like what?'

'About Jamie? Who were those men in suits? They looked like bodyguards.'

She hurried to try and put Mona off the scent. 'Oh, I don't know. Just some guys who were passing, I think.'

'Well, for guys who were *just passing* they hang around a lot. And they talk to Jamie a lot.'

'He's probably just thanking them.'

'He's not some secret undercover boss, or anything?' Mona grinned. 'Because if he's secretly the CEO of the NHS then I think we need to enlighten him about a few things.'

Freya laughed. 'Jamie? No!'

'I just think it's strange, that's all. They even wear those earpiece things…like Secret Service guys.'

Thank goodness she didn't blush as she'd used

to. 'Really? That's weird. But, no, Jamie is just a midwife. Honestly.'

Mona nodded, watching her. 'Okay.' She got up and went to the door, put her hand on the handle. 'You know, I still don't understand why you two aren't together. You obviously slept together, and you seem to get on. So what's keeping you apart?'

Freya shrugged. 'He's a temp. He'll be leaving soon—there's no point.'

'But Sarah from HR told me that they've offered him a permanent post, which he's accepted.'

That was news to Freya. Why hadn't Jamie told her? That he was planning on sticking around for her and the babies?

'I didn't know.'

'It's clear he has feelings for you.'

Her smile was tinged with sadness. 'For the babies, not me.'

'You really think that? I've seen the way his eyes shine when he talks about you. The way his face lights up.'

'He talks about me?'

Mona nodded. 'Frequently. He *cares* about you. You must see it.'

She cared about him, too. Probably more than she should. But she'd been holding back. Afraid of showing any of it. Alone in the day, she dreamed about what it would be like to be with him, and at night her dreams were filled with his smiling face and his steaming hot kisses.

No wonder she woke up cranky. She couldn't have what she wanted the most. Was afraid to let herself have him in case she lost him.

'It's complicated.'

Mona laughed. 'When isn't it? Look, I've got to go, but he'll be in later. Do me a favour and be nice to him. He's doing his best, but you're a bloody expert at keeping people at a distance. Let him care for you, Freya. He's not Mike.'

No. She knew that.

'It's difficult.'

'"*Tis better to have loved and lost, than never to have loved at all.*" Who was it who said that? Was it Shakespeare?'

'I never was any good at English.'

'Me neither.' Mona opened the door. 'But we're very good at chemistry!'

And she gave Freya a tiny wave before she headed off to do her shift.

Freya lay there on the bed, thinking over all the things her friend had said. Jamie was staying on permanently. He had feelings for her. She had feelings for him. The babies would be here soon.

We could be a family.

If she were only brave enough to let it happen.

Was it better to love someone and then lose them than not to love at all?

It sounded to her like devastation. And Jamie's mother had died of it.

Could she let her babies grow to love their father in the knowledge that he would desert them at some point? And would her babies one day leave her too?

But the temptation to give in, to try it, to accept the love and care that Jamie clearly wanted to give her, was extremely potent. The proximity of all that imagined happiness was intoxicating.

If she gave herself the chance to explore that happiness, to cast all her concerns to one side and just live in the moment with him, what would that be like?

Her heart soared at the idea. At the hope. At the possibility of such happiness.

Didn't she deserve it?

No matter how short-lived?

Jamie opened the door to Freya's room and stopped, frozen in place, when he saw how she looked.

Out of bed. Getting dressed.

Smiling. No. *Beaming*.

'What's happened?'

'I've been told I can go home and start my maternity leave. As long as I rest.'

He frowned and went to the end of her bed, picked up her chart and began to read it. 'The bleeding's stopped?'

'For almost a day now.'

'And your blood pressure is down?'

'Almost to normal levels. I can get out of here. You've no idea how much I've longed to hear that.'

'Well, I know how much you've been bugging your consultant about it, so I have a fair idea.'

He smiled. These last few days had been hard for her.

'All this bed rest… I could have done it at home in the first place. There was no need for me to have taken up a bed.'

'There was *every* need. Here, I've brought you a milkshake.' He passed her the drink he'd bought from the café downstairs. 'Why don't you sit down? I'll do your packing for you.'

She held up her hand. 'No, thank you! I don't need you seeing all my knickers and things.'

He smiled, picking up a pair of unflattering maternity pants. 'Why ever not? I've seen—no, *tasted*—what's underneath.'

And then he grinned, because he saw how flustered that comment made her.

She snatched them from him. 'I haven't been allowed to do anything for myself for days now. At least let me do this.'

'Okay.' He sank onto her bed and watched her busily pack her holdall, the excitement in her eyes at finally being able to leave the hospital almost palpable. 'I hope when you get home you do actually rest.'

'I'm fine. I've been discharged. There are things I have to get done. The nursery isn't ready and—'

'Then I'll help you. Tell me what needs doing and I'll get it sorted.'

She stopped to look at him. 'How will you have the time? Now that you're a *permanent* member of staff? Yes, I know about that. Why didn't you tell me?'

'I was waiting until I'd actually signed the contract. Which I did about twenty minutes ago. So here I am. Telling you. Don't change the subject.'

'I'm not.'

'You did. Now, what do you need help with in the nursery?'

'I've ordered two cribs, which are going to be delivered, and some furniture—all of which will need building.'

He nodded. 'I'll do it.'

'I can do it. I'm not helpless.'

'I know you're not, Freya, but you are still meant to be resting.'

'Don't I get *any* say in this?'

He thought for a moment, then smiled. 'No.'

She smiled back. 'You're infuriating, you know?'

Jamie nodded, happy to be so if it meant she was taking it easy. He had no doubt that if he let her go home without supervision she'd be up ladders and cleaning and painting and building wardrobes and putting herself straight back into a hospital bed. He couldn't allow that to happen.

'How are you getting home?'

'Mum's coming over on the bus, then we're using my car to drive back. It's been in the staff car park ever since my fall on the ice.'

'Okay.' He knew her mum would take good care of her. 'I'm on shift now until seven, but I'll pop round straight after—see what needs doing and formulate a plan.'

'You don't need to babysit me.'

'I know.' He stood up and dropped a kiss onto her cheek.

She looked a little startled. 'I'm a grown woman.'

He smiled again, as his mind handily provided him with flashbacks to that steamy night many moons ago. 'I *know*.'

'Stop it.'

'What?'

'Remembering what we did.'

'I'm not allowed to remember?'

'Not that, no.'

'Why?'

'Because of the way it makes you smile. The way you look like you hope it will happen again.'

He stood up and stepped between her and the holdall. 'Would that be a bad thing?'

She was breathing heavily, and licked her lips. She tried her hardest not to look at his lips, but failed.

'Yes.'

'We wouldn't know unless we tried.'

She licked her lips again, bit the lower one and then looked away. Then back again.

'I'm on bed rest.'

'We could be in bed.' He smiled.

She swallowed. 'Please don't, Jamie.'

'Why?'

'Because we *can't*!'

'Who says?'

'The consultant. He said no sex.'

Well, wasn't *that* interesting? Freya herself wasn't saying no. She wasn't turning him down because *she* didn't want to, but because it was a strict order from her consultant.

He smiled, feeling a swell of joy not only in his heart, but elsewhere too.

'I can wait.' He paused to stare at her, then laid his hand on her arm, stilling her, drawing her close. 'Won't you give us a chance to be together?' he whispered.

Her eyes looked up at him, full of conflict, yearning and desire.

Until he bent his head and kissed her.

CHAPTER SEVEN

His lips were soft, gentle. It was the most tender kiss. As his lips met hers it was as if the world slowed. Everything around her faded into nothingness, and all that mattered, all she could feel, was his lips pressed against her own. She forgot her scars, forgot her fears.

Tenderness. Heat. Her heart racing inside her chest…pounding away within the cage that contained it.

He's kissing me!

She'd thought about what it would be like to kiss him again, without hiding behind masks and anonymity.

She knew him now. Knew who Jamie was. *What* he was. He'd become her friend as well as her colleague, and somehow, without her realising how, he had wormed his way into her affections. She cared for him. Worried about him. Feared for their future.

And she had wondered what it might be like

for them both if their lives were different. If he weren't heir to the throne of some faraway kingdom, and if she weren't the woman who hid behind the scars on her face.

And now he's kissing me.

She felt herself sink further into his embrace. Felt her body press up against his. God, she needed this! Needed *him*.

Freya had never imagined losing herself to something so wonderful as this.

But it felt so right. It felt so *good*.

She was almost dizzy with all the sensations running rampant through her system, with all the emotions she was experiencing. What was it doing to her blood pressure?

I need to breathe.

She pulled back, looked at him, her eyes dazed with confusion.

'You kissed me.'

'Yes.' His eyes shone darkly, with a heat in them she had never noticed before.

'Why?' It was a whisper.

'Because I needed to.'

'Needed?'

A smile. 'Wanted.'

'Me?'

Another smile. Broader this time. 'Of *course* you. When will you start to believe that?'

Her words caught in her throat for a moment, a painful lump of disbelief that she had to swallow down, blinking rapidly to stop the tears from falling.

'I see you, Freya. Who you are. I see the woman who stands before me today and she's the bravest, strongest, most wonderful woman I know.'

'I don't…'

'You keep comparing yourself to who you used to be. I don't know who you used to be, or what you looked like before, and I don't need to know. That was the past. What matters is the present, the *now*, and the woman before me is beautiful. She is caring and loving, fragile yet strong and courageous. As beautiful on the inside as she is on the outside. That's who I see.'

He tucked a strand of her hair behind her ear.

'But…'

'No buts. No whys or maybes. Just accept it. Can you accept the fact that I have feelings for you and that I'd like us to be more than just friends?'

It was everything she could possibly want to hear. Everything she's thought she'd never hear. And here he was. This man. This drop-dead gorgeous, handsome *prince* was saying it to her!

And suddenly she felt afraid. Afraid of what it all meant. If she accepted it—if she let him in—

then wouldn't she be making herself vulnerable all over again?

But she was teetering on the edge of a giant abyss and she wanted to fall for him. Wanted to believe so much!

Her heartbeat pounded in her ears. She felt hot and dizzy with it all. But she wasn't ill. Just lovesick. And she wanted that happiness, even if it was just for a short while. She'd accept it and have him for as long as she could have him.

'I can.'

Hesitantly she smiled at him, watching as his face lit up.

He let out a heavy breath and beamed at her, before pulling her back into his embrace. 'Then let's get you safely home and we'll take it from there.'

It was strange to be back home. Her mum put on a pot of decaffeinated coffee to brew. Freya sat on the couch, her feet up, cradling her mug.

'I think Jamie and I are going to give things a go.'

It felt odd to say it. *Jamie and I.*

Her mum smiled at her over her own mug. 'Really? Oh, I'm so pleased to hear that. I really am.'

'We don't know what's going to happen, but we're going to take it a day at a time. It's all we *can* do, really.'

'Stop downplaying it, Freya. You're already making it sound like it's doomed before it starts.'

'I'm just being realistic.'

'No, you're trying to protect yourself before you get hurt and it won't work that way. If you are going to give it a try with Jamie then you've got to be in it wholeheartedly. One hundred per cent. Not with one foot already out of the door.'

'You think that's what I'm doing?'

Her mum put her mug down and came over to sit beside her. Took her hand in her own. 'I know that's what you're doing. But Jamie's different. He's honourable and kind and I think he cares deeply about you. You can't play with his feelings because you're scared. Be in it totally, give everything of your heart, one hundred per cent, or don't give anything at all.'

Tears began to sting her eyes. 'I want to be with him.'

'Then do it.'

'But what if—?'

'No what ifs, Freya. No fear. You are having two babies with this man, and whether it works or not he will be in your life until your last day on this earth. So make it work. Give him your whole heart, not half of it.'

The tears began to fall. 'I think I might love him.'

Her mum was tearing up too.

'Then you both have my blessing.'

She leaned forward and kissed Freya on the cheek, then pulled her into a hug.

Casey Benson looked calm. She was sitting in her hospital bed, serenely tapping a message into her mobile phone. But then again, Jamie mused, Casey had been through this three times before. She was an experienced mother.

'Hi, Casey. I'm Jamie, and I'm going to be your midwife today.'

She turned and smiled, her smile freezing slightly when she saw him. 'I get *you*?'

He nodded. 'You do.'

'For when I give birth?'

'That's the plan!'

'Oh.'

She looked a little perturbed, and he wondered if she was feeling uncomfortable at having a man deliver her child.

'Is that all right?'

'Yes! Course it is, it's just…'

'Yes?'

She blushed. 'You're very attractive.'

Well, that was very flattering, but he didn't understand why that should be a problem.

'An attractive man down at my—' She stopped and blushed again. Her face going very red.

He tried to change the subject, feeling amused. 'Are you here alone today?'

'I always do this alone.'

He saw on her file that she was married. 'Is your husband at work?'

'You could say that. He's in the Antarctic.'

'Oh, really? Doing what?'

'He's part of a research team studying the biodiversity of a special organism, or some such thing. He hopes to be back when this one is about two months old.'

'No other family who can be with you?'

'There is, but I'm happy to do this myself. It never takes long—they usually pop out after an hour or two. I'll be home in a few hours.'

'Who's babysitting the others?'

'Mum is. She's not very good with blood and gore, but she's an absolute whizz with spilt milk and baby dribble, so she's keeping an eye on the troops.'

'Glad to hear it. So it's just you and me, then. Unless you'd like a chaperone?'

She smiled at him over her mobile. 'Just you and me is fine.'

Casey had been right. She did labour easily. Though her contractions were showing up good and strong on the trace she remained calm, breathing easily through each of them as she leaned over the back of her bed, her knees on the mattress.

'You're doing brilliantly, Casey.'

Casey beckoned him over. 'Come and join me for a selfie. Otherwise no one is going to believe I had *you* deliver my baby.'

He capitulated, and put his head close to hers for a photo, smiling as the camera on her phone clicked the two of them together.

'You still all right with just the gas and air?'

'Absolutely!' She settled back on her haunches whilst she waited for the next contraction. 'Still all systems go here. Though, if I'm honest with you, I can't believe I'm back here, doing this again. I swore the last time that Benji was going to be my last baby, yet here I am.'

'Does your husband get to come home often?'

'Every six months. He gets home for about four weeks and then he goes off again. And obviously, because we haven't seen each other in all that time, we're very keen to see each other as much as we can, if you get my drift, and that usually results in me peeing on another of those ruddy sticks. Mind you, I love being a mum. I love all my kids—we have such a great time.'

'Do they miss their dad? What with him not being around?'

'Of course they do! They play up every now and again, but don't all children? They know their dad loves them, and that he's off doing some very special scientific work, and it's good for them to see that their dad is dedicated and works hard for a cause he believes in. It's good moral grounding for them.'

'It must be hard for him, too. Being away from his children?'

She nodded. 'It is. But he absolutely adores what he does, and I don't think he could be away from them unless he did. Why would he lose all that time he could have with them if he was stuck somewhere hating what he did? No, it's good he has that passion. Do you have kids?'

He smiled. 'I have two on the way.'

'Twins, huh? Wow. But I imagine you'll be the same. You must love what you do? Because when they're born…when they're finally here and you hold them in your own arms…you can't imagine spending any time away from them. Missing any of it. Not unless you love what you do.'

He nodded. She was right. He wanted to spend as much time as he possibly could with his babies when they came. And if at some point he got called away to be King of Majidar that would be his crisis point.

Because he could *never* imagine himself wanting to do that. Could not imagine himself being stuck inside a glittering palace, getting bogged down in politics and laws, stuff he didn't care for, when instead he could be with his children. Doing a job he adored.

Majidar was never meant to be his. Ilias should have had his own heirs. He was a midwife. It had always been his calling. His vocation. He'd never wanted to rule, but it was the family he had been born into. And he felt a responsibility there, too.

The people of Majidar expected him to be their next King. And he knew, because it had been reported to him, that his people were *proud* of him for following his passion, for working far away from them in another country, bringing life into the world. But they knew he would come back. They *expected* him to come back.

But he wanted to be with his children. And Freya.

Unexpectedly, he had built a life here. Was putting down roots for the first time ever. And it was exciting and thrilling and the most terrifying thing he had ever done.

But it also felt like the *right* thing.

Knowing he would have to leave at some point, knowing he would have to walk away from them, was killing him inside.

Casey pulled herself back up over the bed railing and began to breathe heavily. 'Okay, let's do this.'

'I'm ready when you are.'

* * *

Casey gave birth to a healthy seven-pound, four-ounce baby girl that she called Francesca.

Jamie escorted her through to Postnatal for a little while and, as she'd predicted, waved her on her way home a few hours after that.

She'd given him a lot to think about, and he wondered if she'd made light of her situation at home. It had to be hard for her, living as a single parent, with her husband away for long periods of time.

Would that be Freya's life too? Stuck here in England alone? Knowing that he was away, and knowing that he'd put his *duty* to his country before his duty to his own children?

Casey was able to do it because she knew her husband was passionate about what he did, and she valued the life lessons she could show her children—that their dad was working hard at something he believed in. That he was doing it for *them*.

Would Freya be able to say the same to their two boys? Jamie *did* believe in the honour and privilege that it would be to sit on his country's throne, but would he be able to like himself for doing something he didn't actually want to do? Forcing himself out of duty?

He arrived at Freya's flat bright and early,

knocking on her door and waiting for her to answer.

She opened it and he held up his box. 'I've brought tools.'

She smiled at him. 'Milkshakes or chocolates are my preferred gifts.'

'Maybe, but milkshakes and chocolates can't build bedroom furniture, can they?' He stepped past her, then stopped, turned, smiled and lowered his head to kiss her. 'Almost forgot this part,' he whispered, his lips closing over hers.

He'd missed her. Even more so since spending time with Casey. He felt the need to be with her. Her and the babies. Whilst he could. Her lips were full, soft and warm. She was comforting to him. It made him feel good just to be with her, and already he could feel his cares and worries being soothed away.

He wanted more. Could feel his body awakening to her touch, her presence. But more was forbidden. Which made the idea of it all the more desirable, and he had to pull back, bite his lip and just look at her with adoration and maddening frustration.

'Has everything arrived?'

'It's all in the nursery, awaiting your attention.'

'Good.'

She stared back at him, licked her lips, and he tracked every motion. The way her tongue swept over her lips, wetting them, leaving them glistening, before slipping back into her mouth.

'Can I make you a drink?'

He let out a sigh, imagining what that tongue could do to his body. 'Tea, please.'

He watched her head off to the kitchen and forcibly pushed aside his very sinful thoughts of all the things he wanted to do to her. That would have to wait. They had time. Time, at least, was on their side.

'I thought it might snow.' He followed her and watched her make the tea. 'They've forecast it in the paper.'

Freya laughed cynically. 'Let me tell you something about England, Jamie. They *always* forecast snow. They give us dire warnings every year, but we never get it. We can barely manage a frost down here, near the coast. It's very disappointing, actually.'

He smiled. 'This time last year I was working in Edinburgh, and we had snow. First time I'd ever experienced a heavy snowfall and it was wonderful.'

'Well, you'd better keep a hold of that memory, because you probably won't get it again.' She handed him his tea, smiling. 'Shall we get to it?'

'I'd love to. But apparently there's furniture that needs building.' He smiled.

She smiled back. 'That's what I meant.'

'You can supervise. And pass me things.' He pointed at her. 'No heavy lifting.'

Freya saluted him. 'Yes, sir.'

'Orders from your consultant.'

'I get it—don't worry. Are you sure you don't want something to eat before we start?'

He turned to look at her, devilment in his eyes. 'Freya, what I want to eat is, unfortunately, not on the menu at this moment in time.'

The instructions for the two cots seemed to be written in gibberish, and the pictures showing where to place the locking nuts didn't seem all that clear either. It took over an hour to do the first cot, through a process of elimination, but by the time he'd started the second he actually felt he knew what he was doing.

Freya sat beside him in a rocking chair, reading a book about what to expect in the first year of their child's life. She looked so cute, rocking away, one hand resting on her ample stomach, intensely concentrating on the words. He sat and watched her for a moment, quite unable to believe that this was his family now.

'Good book?'

She closed it and wiggled her eyebrows. 'Scary book. There seems so much to watch out for and worry about.'

'Like what?'

'Like colic, whooping cough, vaccinations and sterilising everything to within an inch of its life! What if they choke on something? What if I wean them too early and it does them more harm than good?' She let out a sigh. 'Being a mum seemed so much easier when it was just hypothetical.'

He could see that she was feeling nervous and needed reassurance. 'We'll be absolutely fine. We can do this. Thousands do.'

'And thousands of parents end up in A&E with their babies—we both know that. They get gastroenteritis and need rehydration drips and monitoring, or they swallow some coin or a marble or a little toy gun—I don't know, *something*—and they need an operation.'

He went to kneel beside her and took her hands in his. 'We can't protect them from everything.'

'But we're their parents. We're meant to protect them from things that will cause them harm!'

'You can't protect them from illness. Germs will get in no matter what you do. And, yes, they might swallow something they shouldn't. I believe I swallowed a small plastic camel when I was two years old, but here I am, absolutely fine and without trauma to my system. It's okay to worry, Freya. It's part of being a parent.'

'But I never thought I'd get the chance at this and now I am! And it's getting closer now, and I'm just worried that I'll get it all wrong!'

'Every mother worries. This is natural. Let's focus our energies on things we can control—like baby names, for instance. Have you had any thoughts on what you might want to call them?'

She let out a sigh and he saw a small smile begin to emerge as she focused on happier things. 'I quite like the name Samuel.'

He mused on it. 'Samuel MacFadden. That sounds like a good strong name.'

She smiled. 'Samuel Al Bakhari. I'm going to give them your surname.'

He sat back on his heels, pleasantly surprised. And honoured. 'You are?'

'And I figured if you let me pick their first names, then you could pick their middle names. Something Arabic? So they get a name from both our cultures?'

'Wow… I don't quite know what to say.' The gesture meant a lot to him.

'Just suggest some good names!'

He smiled back at her, stroking her beautiful face and staring into her eyes.

They decided upon Samuel Dawoud and James Kadin.

'Good, strong names.'

'For good, strong boys.' She rubbed her tummy. 'They'll be here soon.'

He squeezed her hands. 'And we'll be ready for them.'

Once the cots were up, and Jamie had powered through constructing a wardrobe, a baby-changing station and a set of drawers, Freya cooked them both something to eat.

It was wonderful to have Jamie there with her, now that she was determined to step forward into the future with him at her side, instead of fighting him every inch of the way. Watching him work on the bedroom furniture, seeing how careful he was, how focused, making sure everything was put together correctly and securely, made her feel warm inside.

'I can't wait to see them in those cots.'

She smiled. 'Me too.'

'Can't wait to see their little faces. Hold them. Love them.'

She knew exactly what he meant. She felt it too.

Passing him a bowl of pasta, she sat down on the couch opposite. 'Thanks for today, Jamie. It feels good to see the nursery taking shape. Makes me feel like I'm a bit more prepared.'

'I'm glad. I'd do anything to make this easier for you.'

'It must be difficult for you too. Not knowing what's ahead?'

He nodded. 'I don't want to screw this up. Us… The twins… Majidar…'

'I never wanted to come between you and your country, Jamie. You have to know that.'

'Of course I do.'

'I just feel like…'

'Like what?'

'Like I'm making you choose. And I know I won't win.'

He put the pasta down. Sat beside her. Kissed her on the forehead. 'This isn't your fault. You're not making me do anything I don't want to.'

'But you have a responsibility to your people. A million of them. I'm just one. Soon to be three. I can't compete with that. I don't want to think of the day when you'll have to make that decision.'

His eyes darkened as he felt her pain. 'I don't want to leave you. You know that?'

She nodded.

Jamie let out a heavy sigh. 'We can't worry about that yet. It could be decades away. Let's consider brighter, better things.' He thought for a moment. 'What do you want to do over Christmas?'

Christmas? She hadn't really thought about it. She'd figured she'd be spending it in the normal way. 'I'll be at my mum's house.'

'I'm scheduled to work over Christmas. The

afternoon shift from two p.m. But I wondered…
well, I *hoped* that maybe we could spend the
morning together?'

'Oh… Okay… Well, why don't you come to
Mum's? It'll give you both an opportunity to
get to know each other a bit more and we'll get
to share the day together. We eat at midday, so
you'll get lunch.'

He smiled and nodded. 'Sounds good. I'd love
that—thank you.'

'I'll let Mum know there'll be an extra mouth
to feed!'

Freya felt good about that. This would be her
last Christmas without children. Maybe next year
she and Jamie would be living together? Inviting
her mum over to their place? Cooking for her instead? And there would be the joy of watching
the babies rip open their presents. Would they
be toddling by then? Crawling? Making mischief
between the pair of them? Babbling away in their
own little twins' language?

The idea of it made her smile. Made her feel
warm and happy. Her future with Jamie might
be uncertain, but whilst he was here they would
make good memories together. Memories they
would both cherish. Every moment would be precious.

Life was changing—and for the better. She
couldn't quite believe she'd resisted this so much!

Look at how well she and Jamie got along! All she'd needed to do was give him a chance. Give *them* a chance. And, even though she still felt apprehensive about the future, everything was looking much brighter now.

Maybe they *could* do this?

Together.

'We're going out.'

Freya frowned at Jamie. She'd just opened the door to him, expecting to invite him in for them to spend the evening together the way they usually did—watching a movie, eating popcorn, that kind of thing. She hadn't been expecting to go out, and she was wearing jogging bottoms and a maternity tee shirt that was having difficulty stretching over her twins-filled abdomen.

'What?'

'I've arranged something special. Just for you. So get dressed—we're heading into town.'

'Into town? Oh, no, I really don't think that I could—'

He pressed a finger to her lips, silencing her with a smile. 'Trust me.'

Freya stared back at him. Going into town was not her favourite thing. She'd done it a few times after the attack. It had been part of her therapy—heading out with her counsellor to show that she was okay being around crowds of people.

She'd been in a crowd of people when Mike had thrown the acid at her. It had happened in town. On the main street. He'd been lucky it hadn't hit anyone else and scarred them too. For a long time she'd been afraid to go out. Had almost become agoraphobic. Her counsellor had worked on exposing her gradually, getting her back out into the world.

It had been a long, difficult road, but one she had accomplished with much pride, even standing in the very spot on which the attack had happened, her eyes closed, breathing everything in—the familiar sounds of people all around her, the faint music from a clothing store playing far away, a busker a little further along, the aroma of freshly brewed coffee, the ringing of the church bells, the hustle and bustle of life all around her.

She'd done it. It had been fine. Until she'd opened her eyes.

Then she'd seen it. The stares of people passing her by. Had watched them notice her scarred face, seen the looks of repulsion, the pity, the sympathy, the recognition of who she was—that girl from the news who was attacked.

Her counsellor had told her not to worry about other people's reactions, but that had been easy for her to say—she hadn't been the one with a ruined face. It had been horrible to be looked at so differently.

Freya had always been pretty. Had always been aware that people looked at her with appreciation. That they'd wanted to know her, be her friend. She'd never had to try too hard with her looks, hadn't needed loads of make-up or anything like that. A natural beauty—wasn't that what everyone had said?

It had been torture to see that change. To look in the mirror and see what everyone else saw. Her face told her story. Her past relationship, her pain, her journey to recovery. Every operation, every painful skin graft—all there on her face for the world to judge. She would always be 'the acid girl'.

It was easier not to expose herself to people like that. To work nights, to order online, to keep to her small group of family and friends and the patients she saw on shift.

She had to admit that her patients had all been fine with her. No one had reacted with shock or pity. One or two had asked her what had happened, but the majority had decided it wasn't any of their business and hadn't asked at all.

Perhaps she needed to let the rest of the world have that chance?

'What have you got planned?' she asked nervously.

'It's a surprise.'

'I don't like surprises. Besides, I'm meant to

be resting,' she added, trying to use her pregnancy as one last grip on the door.

'I've taken all that into consideration.' He stepped into her flat and closed the door behind him. 'Now, go and get dressed.'

'Jamie, the town…for me, it's—'

He pulled her towards him and held her tightly. 'I know. I *do*. But we won't be going anywhere near that part of it and I'll be with you every step of the way.'

What had he got planned? She didn't like surprises. Surprises were bad news.

Reluctantly she rummaged in her wardrobe for anything that might fit her and found a pair of maternity jeans and a pink hoodie that said *I'm Doing Nine Months Inside.*

Then she brushed her hair, put it up into a ponytail, added a bit of mascara to her lashes and some lip gloss, a quick spritz of perfume and stood in front of the mirror. Psyching herself up for this 'surprise'.

When she was ready she headed out, grabbing her handbag. 'Will I do?'

His face lit up in a smile. 'You look perfect.'

'Where are you taking me?'

'I told you—it's a surprise.' He got her coat and helped her put it on, slipping her arms into the sleeves, and then grabbed her long, woolly scarf and wrapped it gently around her neck, before dropping a soft kiss on her nose.

She followed him down to his car and he opened the door for her, closing it again once she was safely inside.

Butterflies gathered in her belly as he drove her towards town. They could be going *anywhere*. To do *anything*! She was meant to be resting—which was why Jamie had been spending every spare moment with her when he wasn't on shift. How he got any sleep and managed to function, she had no idea, but he must be power-napping or something, because he always seemed wide awake when he was with her.

And she liked it that he was spending this time with her. It was good for them. Snuggling on the sofa, holding hands, each kiss he gave her heartfelt and meaningful, warming her, making her feel safe and secure and loved.

Oh, there'd been times when she'd wanted a whole lot more! But they were both on strict instructions. No sex until the babies were born! And, as they were determined to keep the twins inside her for as long as they could, they were both being extremely diligent about that rule.

Jamie drove them through the streets towards town, and Freya had to admit it looked really pretty at night. The Christmas lights were up, adorning most of the streets in the city centre,

Christmas music was being played, and everyone seemed to be in a happy, relaxed mood. Perhaps everyone was feeling goodwill to all men?

Jamie parked in a small service road to the rear of one of the big shopping centres.

Where on earth were they?

Jamie got out, walked around the outside of the car and then opened her door. 'Madam?'

She smiled nervously. 'Where are we? What are we doing?'

'I need my guys to watch the car, so I've parked here; it means my security looks a little less conspicuous. And I think you'll find that we'll be met in just a moment.'

He pressed a buzzer beside a set of double doors and instantly they were opened by a woman wearing a pretty blue dress and a name tag that read *'Michelle'.*

'Mr Bakhari? Miss MacFadden? Good evening and welcome to The Nesting Site.'

The Nesting Site? She'd read about that store in the local paper when it had opened up a few years ago. It was a stylish baby store, selling everything from plain muslin squares right through to the most hi-tech buggy anyone could possibly hope to purchase. It was exclusive—and a bit pricey, too. She'd heard some of her patients, when they'd come in to give birth, talking about browsing there, just to look at the beautiful things.

'I have a lift on hold, waiting for us.'

Michelle stood back to let them in and Freya breathed in the woman's perfume as she passed her by, feeling completely underdressed in her jeans and hoodie. She leant in towards Jamie for security and comfort, and felt better when he took her hand in his and give it a squeeze.

Michelle was looking at her with a polite smile. 'How many months are you?'

'Seven and a half, but it's twins, so...'

Michelle nodded, as if she understood perfectly. 'I had twins. One of each. Do you know what flavours you're expecting?'

'Two boys.'

Michelle smiled. 'Two princes. How wonderful!'

Freya looked at Jamie in shock. Did this woman know *who* and *what* Jamie was? She'd thought he didn't tell anyone that. But Jamie just smiled enigmatically at her and said nothing.

The lift doors pinged open and Michelle invited them in to the amazing store.

Freya sucked in a breath at all the beautiful things she could see—cribs with white lace curtains, the most beautiful rocking chairs, baby clothes in all manner of colours and designs, from plain white with gold embroidery through to brightly patterned Babygros in pinks and blues and the palest of palettes.

Michelle indicated a large reclining chair, stuffed with cushions, for Freya to sit down upon—which she did, wondering just what was about to happen here.

'I've arranged for us to have the store to ourselves, and for personal shoppers to bring us anything we wish to see. We don't have any clothes yet for the little ones, and I'd like us to get a few things.' Jamie smiled and squeezed her hand once more.

'Jamie, you didn't have to do this. I could have ordered online, like I always do.'

'I thought it would be better to see the items in person, before we buy. And I know you don't like crowds, so we have the place to ourselves. Now, what sort of thing should we look at first?'

'How about their going-home outfits?' Michelle suggested, snapping her fingers at some staff who must be were hidden away beyond Freya's eyeline. 'Would you like some tea? I can have a tray brought in.'

She almost felt dizzy with the possibility of it all.

Was this what it felt like to be a princess?

A princess in a hoodie and jeans...

CHAPTER EIGHT

'JAMIE, THIS FEELS WEIRD.' She leant over to whisper to him.

He smiled at her. 'Why?'

'All these people running around after me. Fetching and carrying. It's not right.'

'It's what *you* do when you're at work. Don't you look after your pregnant mothers? Fetching them cups of tea? Getting them epidurals or pethidine or gas and air? Don't you rub their backs and mop their heads with cool flannels when they need it? Hold their hands?'

She could understand his point. But that was different, surely? That was her *job*. Her patients needed her to do that because that was what she was trained to do. It was what she was there for.

'It's what they're here for, Freya,' Jamie said, echoing her thought process. 'It's what they're paid to do.'

'It just doesn't feel right to be on the receiving end of it, that's all.'

'Enjoy it whilst you can. When Samuel and James get here you'll look back on this moment and wonder why you didn't take full advantage of getting to put your feet up for a short while.'

She smiled as she imagined her babies in her arms. Who would they look like? Would they be dark-haired, like Jamie? Or blonde, like her? Would they have his intense midnight-dark eyes or her blue ones? Would they be happy, giggly babies? Or cry all the time with colic?

It was getting so close now, and she couldn't wait to hold them in her arms. To feel their little bodies snuggled up close to hers. She was looking forward to breastfeeding, if she could, although she worried about producing enough milk for both of them. She knew her body was designed to produce as much milk as the babies needed, but she couldn't stop worrying. Fretting about this and that. All the *what ifs* and all the horrors that might befall them.

She knew it was a normal part of being a new parent. She and Jamie were about to take on a huge responsibility and that they, more than anyone else, had uncertain futures.

I can't think about that now. I told myself I wouldn't.

The personal shoppers arrived, pushing a small clothes rail from which hung a plethora of baby clothes on tiny hangers. She went through them one by one, holding them, touching them. Laughing and smiling with Jamie as they imagined their sons dressed in each item and cooing over the small size of each piece.

She picked out baby vests and Babygros, tee shirts and tiny pairs of trousers. There were the most gorgeous pairs of baby shoes and trainers, pure white scratch mitts and the cutest knitted hats that looked like raccoons and foxes. She chose them both a winter snow suit, and picked out towels with white stripes that were adorned with tiny white sheep, and a gorgeous set of soft cherrywood brushes for their hair.

Michelle suggested a range of handmade bibs that were more like neckerchiefs, and then they moved on to car seats, and a double buggy that they both practised putting up and collapsing down. Freya chose a V-shaped pillow to assist with breastfeeding support, and a cute bedroom thermometer that looked like an owl. Plain and patterned fitted sheets and cellular blankets went onto the purchase pile. Then there were all the toys—teddy bears and rattles and soothers.

As each item was scanned Freya began to feel a little queasy. She saw the total totting up but, glancing at Jamie, she saw he was totally unfazed and realised that cost was not a concern for him. How nice it must be, she thought, not to have to worry about the pennies.

'And where shall we deliver this?' Michelle asked.

Jamie gave them her address and arranged a time for delivery tomorrow, promising Freya that the men would bring everything up to her flat and pack it away for her, so that she didn't have to do a thing.

'Oh, no—I'd like to do it, if that's okay.' She very much wanted to go through everything by herself. Sorting out where to put the clothes and how to organise everything in the wardrobes that Jamie had put up the other day.

'Just the clothes,' Jamie agreed. 'You're meant to be resting.'

Michelle escorted them back through the store, down into the lift and back to their car, waving at them as they drove off, with a big smile on her face.

'Well, if she works on commission I think we've just bought enough to give her the rest of the year off,' Freya joked.

Jamie laid his hand on hers. 'Did you enjoy it?'

She smiled. 'I did. You were right—it was lovely to actually see the items in person, rather than online. Some of those clothes were just so *dinky*!'

He laughed. 'They were, weren't they?'

Freya out a long sigh. 'So, are we going back home now?'

'I thought we could go and get something to eat, if that's okay?'

She thought of the crowds, and her mood dipped slightly. 'What did you have in mind?'

'How about pizza?'

Oh, yes! 'You read my mind.'

Jamie parked the car by the marina and left the engine on, keeping them warm as they ate their pizza. The boats were lit with security lights and bobbed about on the gently rocking waves as the wind whipped across the bay, biting at any exposed flesh on passers-by.

'Thanks for tonight, Jamie. It was amazing—it really was.'

'Once you got over what it felt like to be looked after for a change?'

She laughed. 'I guess.'

He peered out of the window. 'Still no snow.'

'I told you.'

'Yes, you did.' He wiped at his mouth and fingers with a napkin, before closing the lid on his pizza. 'That was delicious.'

'The pizza? Or me being right?'

He smiled at her. 'Both. And I wouldn't have it any other way.'

Wouldn't he? She knew this situation wasn't ideal for either of them. They both wanted the same things for the years ahead. They wanted to stay here in England. But he knew he would have to leave at some point. To be King. It was a dark thought that cast a long shadow over both of them.

'I'm sorry, Jamie.'

He turned to her and frowned. 'For what?'

'For not being able to leave here. For not agreeing to be your wife. I know it's me that's making this difficult for you and that if I just changed my mind then everything would be okay.'

Jamie shook his head. 'I would never force you to do anything. *Never*. I love the fact that you have been honest with me.' He took one of her hands in his and kissed the back of it. 'You were true to yourself. You told me the truth and I appreciate that. It makes what we have all the more special.'

She squeezed his fingers. 'What *do* we have, Jamie? Sometimes I'm not sure of anything.'

'We have a promise to be there for our children together, as much as we can be. To love them, and each other, until we can no longer do so.'

And each other? What did he mean by that? That he loved her? Or that the babies would love each other? That they would have a loving family? What he'd said was ambiguous. It could mean anything. And, although she was desperate to know whether he loved her, she felt at that moment that she couldn't ask him. The words were stuck in her throat.

She nodded. 'I don't want them to miss out on anything.'

'They won't.'

'I don't mean we should spoil them. I mean...' She looked away, out across the bay, past the boats and out to sea, where God only knew what was waiting. 'I mean that they should know just how much they are loved, by *both* of us. Even if one of us isn't there.'

'They will.' Jamie's voice was deep and full of emotion.

She loved it that he cared about this as much as she did. That his love for their babies ran as deeply as hers. Desperately she wanted to grab his hands and beg him never to go. Never to leave them. But she knew she couldn't ask him that. He had a duty. Over a million people would need him one day.

She couldn't make him choose between Majidar and her! He would always resent her for making him do it. So she knew that one day he would have to leave, and the idea of that, as her babies' birth grew closer, was beginning to break her heart.

Her feelings for Jamie had changed and grown. Especially over these last few weeks. Why did they have to be in this situation? Why did he have to be born to such a duty? Why couldn't he just be a midwife? Some random guy whom she'd met one day?

Why did he have to be a prince? Heir to a throne?

Why would she have to break her own heart one day and let go of him?

It wasn't fair.

Christmas morning arrived in the middle of a downpour.

Freya would not let the rain sully her day. It didn't matter. What mattered was that today was a day for family, and that for the first time in for ever she wouldn't be spending it alone with her mum. Jamie would be with them, arriving mid-morning, having lunch with them, before he had to leave for his shift at the hospital.

She hoped he'd like the present she'd got him. It had taken her ages to find something she thought he might like. What did you buy a *prince*—a man who could buy anything?

In the end she'd been rather sneaky, asking the security guys who followed her to get her a picture of Jamie's most successful racehorse so that she could have a painting done. One of her patients was an artist, and she'd commissioned her to do it.

Freya had to admit the painting looked amazing. Jamie's horse, Pride of Jameel, was a magnificent-looking animal, and Susie had painted the stallion standing tall and proud on a sand dune, his black coat gleaming.

As a little something extra—something silly—she'd got him a pair of teddy bears that played a recording of their twins' heartbeats when their bellies were squeezed.

'Merry Christmas, Mum!'

'Merry Christmas, Freya!' Her mum turned and blew her a kiss before turning her attention back to the frying pan. 'Full English for you?'

'Erm…just bacon and eggs, please.'

'What time are we expecting your young man?'

'Around ten, I think.'

'You've told him we don't open our gifts until after lunch?'

Freya nodded.

'And he's okay with turkey?'

'Yes, Mum.'

'What about the sausages? They're pork.'

'If there's anything he doesn't want he'll just leave it.'

'I don't want to offend him.'

'You won't, Mum. Honestly.'

'It's such an important day. I wouldn't want to ruin it.'

She helped her mum prepare all the vegetables,

peel the potatoes and baste the turkey, which was already in the oven. The kitchen was filled with succulent aromas as they made the bread sauce, the cranberry sauce, and her mum's special stuffing. In the background Christmas carols played from the radio, and Freya realised as she sliced and chopped that she had never felt happier. It was Christmas, she was going to be a mother, and she had a man in her life whom she loved.

She'd fought it. Oh, how she'd tried to fight it! But she had to be honest with herself and admit the truth. She loved Jamie. He'd made it impossible for her not to.

Part of her still couldn't quite believe she had made herself that vulnerable again, but the other part—her love for Jamie—kept telling her it didn't matter, because she felt sure he loved her too and that he would never try to hurt her the way that Mike had, that by opening her heart and allowing him in she was not going to get burned this time.

There was only one way Jamie could hurt her, and that was by leaving, but she was being optimistic and trusting in what Jamie had said. They might have *years* together yet. Samuel and James might be grown men before he got called back to Majidar, so why waste all that time being lonely and miserable when they could be together, happy and loved?

The doorbell rang, breaking her thoughts, and instantly a smile lit her face. Wiping her hands on a tea towel, she went to answer the door.

Jamie stood on the doorstep beneath the shadow of a large black umbrella, holding a small sack of Christmas presents in his other hand.

'Merry Christmas!'

He smiled and stepped forward, planting a kiss upon her lips that made her hungry for more. She could have stood there all day, kissing him in the doorway, if it hadn't been for her mum coming to the door.

'Well, let the poor man in, Freya—it's bucketing down out there!'

'Something smells good.'

'It's your lunch. I hope you're hungry?'

He met her gaze. 'Starving.'

Freya could have melted there and then. The heat between them had been growing uncontrollably, and it was a terrible struggle not to let things advance between them physically when it was what they both wanted.

'Come on through. I'll make you a cup of tea.'

'Nope.' He took the bag of presents back from her. 'I'll make the tea. You put your feet up. Just show me where to put these and I'll get right on it.'

Freya showed him where to put the presents

and then allowed him to settle her down on the couch, lifting her feet onto a foot rest.

He leaned over her, his hands either side of her, his face close to her own. 'I've missed you.'

'You saw me just yesterday.' She smiled, glancing down at his soft, sultry lips.

'And I missed you the second I left. I'm so happy to be here with you today. You have no idea.'

How was everything going so right for her? How was she so lucky? To have this—Jamie, the babies, Christmas, the *future*. Just a year or so ago her future had seemed quite lonely, but now…now she had everything she could possibly want. Perhaps it *was* her turn to be happy. She'd had what felt like a lifetime of pain, disappointment and grief. Her luck was turning at last.

Jamie slid onto the couch next to her and she rested her head against his strong, broad shoulder. She sat there feeling content. *Happy*.

CHAPTER NINE

'YOU'VE NOT GOT long now. Just a few more weeks before those babies arrive. What are you planning on doing once they get here?'

Freya frowned at her mum. 'How do you mean?'

'Well I know you're getting the flat ready, and the nursery is all decked out, but do you have any plans to move in together?'

Freya looked at Jamie, unsure. They hadn't talked about this.

'I'd be lying if I said I hadn't thought about the future, but I don't want to push Freya unless she's ready,' Jamie answered diplomatically.

It was scary. Terrifying. But she said it anyway. 'I might be ready.'

He raised an eyebrow, smiling. 'Really?'

'I'll need all the help I can get when the twins are born, and it would make sense, wouldn't it?'

Freya's mum was looking between them. 'What a romantic you are, Freya! You could sound a little more enthusiastic if you're asking him to move in!'

If she'd been able to blush properly she would have. Instead she looked at Jamie uncertainly. 'I'd love you to move in. If *you're* ready?'

Did he know how much it was taking for her to say this?

Jamie put down his knife and fork, dabbed at his mouth with a napkin and then got to his feet, walking around the table to kneel by her side. He took her hand in his and kissed it. 'I'd love to move in.'

Freya's mum clapped her hands together in excitement. 'Oh, yes! What a merry Christmas it is, indeed!'

Jamie embraced Freya in a quick hug, kissed her on the lips and then went back to his seat. 'Let's have a toast.' He raised his glass of juice and waited for Freya and her mum to do the same. 'To moving in and to bright futures.'

'To moving in and to bright futures!'

Their glasses clinked.

Freya had got her mum a scarf, hat and mittens set, along with a couple of books she wanted and some Belgian chocolates to satisfy her sweet tooth.

In return she'd received a gift voucher, some perfume, a new pair of pyjamas and a book in which to record all the twins' milestones as they grew.

'Thanks, Mum.'

'You're welcome, love.'

'Your turn, Jamie.'

Her mum had bought him a bottle of after-shave and a jumper, which he immediately tried on and declared that it fitted perfectly.

'Thank you, Mrs MacFadden.'

He handed Freya's mum an envelope, and when she opened it she realised, to her immense delight, that she'd been given a pass for a spa day at the Franklin Hotel.

'Jamie, that's brilliant—thank you!'

'After all your hard work in the kitchen today, you deserve it.'

'Open this next.'

Freya passed Jamie her present. The painting of his favourite horse, wrapped in bubble wrap and Christmas paper and tied with a huge, sparkly silver bow.

Curious, he began to unwrap it, struggling a little with all the tape Freya had used, until eventually he turned it around to see what it was.

'Freya, that's just *gorgeous*! It looks like Pride of Jameel.'

'It *is*!'

She laughed at the pure delight and amazement on his face, pleased that she could make him so happy—the same way he made *her* feel. This was what it was all about. Moments like these. When you could make the person you loved feel joy.

'How did you manage it?'

'Well, seeing as you've insisted I have bodyguards follow me around, I put them to actual work and told them to get me a photo of your most beloved horse.'

'It's amazing!' He kept admiring it, turning it this way and that to catch the light and admire new aspects of the painting. Then he put it down and kissed her. 'Thank you.'

'There's this, too.' She handed him the wrapped teddy bears.

He opened the gift, smiling when he saw it was two honey-coloured bears.

'Squeeze their tummies.'

He did, and his face broke into a huge smile when he heard the babies' heartbeats, which she'd had recorded at one of her antenatal visits.

'Samuel and James. I'll treasure them. Always.'

Freya felt she could burst with happiness! She hadn't been sure how he'd feel about the gifts, but she was thrilled with how much he liked the painting of his horse. It meant so much to her that he did.

'There's only two gifts left. Both for you, Freya.' Her mum smiled, passing over the gifts.

They were both small boxes. Jewellery-sized boxes. The type that rings came in…

Feeling nervous, Freya accepted the first one and began to unwrap it.

She'd been right. It was a small, red velvet box, shaped like a heart.

What if he was going to ask her to marry him again? Here and now? What would she say?

Sucking in a deep breath, she pushed open the lid.

There, nestled on a cushion of dark blue silk, was a pair of beautiful earrings. Silver, each encircling a beautiful jewel.

'They're platinum, and the jewels are black diamonds. The largest I could find.'

'They're beautiful!'

'Put them in, Freya,' urged her mum.

Part of her felt relief that his gift wasn't a ring. But there was still that second box. There could be a ring in there. It wasn't over yet.

She smiled nervously and put in the earrings, which both her mum and Jamie admired.

'They look beautiful on you, love.'

'Diamonds for my diamond.' Jamie smiled.

She leant over as much as she was able to and kissed him, meeting his gaze and holding it, trying to tell him without words just how much he meant to her and how frightened she was by his next gift.

It had to be the ring in that box, didn't it? And she wanted to say yes, but how could she? When the worst happened and Jamie got called back to Majidar she would have to go with him if she were his wife. It would be expected. But if she said no then she'd be ruining this beautiful day and breaking both their hearts, when right now they were both so happy.

Why had he done this? *Why?*

She felt a small surge of anger inside, irritation flooding her that it was all about to go wrong. She was about to feign a headache, or something, when the front doorbell rang.

Her mum frowned. 'Who on earth could that be? It's Christmas!'

'I'll go,' Jamie said, getting to his feet.

But Freya, feeling the need to escape the anticipation of what was in that tiny box, laid her hand upon his arm, stopping him. 'No. I'll go. You two have been looking after me all day—I need to stretch my legs for a moment.'

It was an excuse, but a welcome one, whoever it was. She just needed time to try and think. To try and decide what to do.

More than anything she would love to be Jamie's wife. To stand by his side with their babies as part of a loving family. But she knew she couldn't put herself under that much scrutiny. The world's press would have a field-day.

'Just coming!' She waddled down the hallway, exhaling loudly as she approached the door. She had no idea who it could be.

Standing before her was a man wearing a long white robe and a traditional *keffiyeh* on his head. He looked sombre, and bowed slightly at her appearance. 'Madam MacFadden. My name is Faiz and I am the personal emissary of His Majesty King Ilias Al Bakhari. It is imperative that I speak with his brother, Prince Jameel.'

Freya froze for a moment as she took in his appearance and his message. Personal emissary? Why would Jamie's brother send a message on Christmas Day? It could hardly be a festive greeting. She was sure that they didn't celebrate Christmas over there in Majidar.

'An emissary?'

Faiz bowed again. 'Time is of the essence. If I may be allowed entry to speak with My Prince?'

Freya blinked rapidly as her brain raced through a thousand and one possibilities. Numb, she moved back and said nothing as Faiz stepped inside and past her.

'Who is it, Freya?' she heard her mum call from the room where moments ago everything had been perfect.

A chill crept over her as she began to suspect

the reason for Faiz's visit. No. It *couldn't* be that. Could it?

Fighting back tears, she followed Faiz to the living room, where he stood just inside the doorway.

Jamie had got to his feet, his face stoic and ashen. 'Faiz?'

'My Prince. I must speak with you privately.'

Jamie glanced at her. The briefest eye contact. He must have seen the horror on her face before he looked away again.

'Anything you have to say, Faiz, can be said in front of everyone here.'

Faiz gave her a considered look, then nodded. 'Your brother has been taken ill. He is in hospital and it is imperative that you return to the kingdom.'

'Ill?'

'It is believed that His Majesty has suffered a stroke.'

Jamie stared at the floor, his body tense, his fists clenched at his side. 'Is Jasmeen with him?'

'The Queen has not left his side.'

'So you need me to return?'

His voice was thick with emotion, and more than anything Freya wanted to go to him and put her arms around him and comfort him, but her own grief kept her glued to the spot.

Jamie was leaving.

Now.

She wasn't ready. She wasn't ready to let him go! They'd only just started to be happy. They'd only just decided to be together. This wasn't fair! What about the babies? It was so close to her due date…he'd miss seeing them born!

'Jamie?' Her voice croaked in a painful whisper of grief.

He couldn't look at her. He just kept staring at the floor.

'Faiz? Are you absolutely sure that I must return?'

'I am not to return without you.'

Her mum hurried over to her and draped an arm around her shoulders. She turned into her mum's body and began to cry.

Behind them, she heard Jamie dismiss Faiz. 'Give me a moment.'

'Yes, My Prince.'

'Freya?'

She couldn't look at him. It hurt too much. She just clutched her mother harder.

'Freya? Please…'

Her mother released her and stepped away. 'I'll be in the kitchen.'

Freya folded her arms around herself and stared at Jamie through her tears. 'You can't go!'

'I must.'

He stepped forward and reached for her, intending to hold her, but she couldn't bear the idea of him touching her. If she let him hold her then she would never let him go.

She stepped back. 'Don't.'

'I never expected this. We were meant to have years...'

'But we both knew that it would happen one day,' she threw back.

'I'm so sorry. I never wanted this.'

She couldn't say anything. Words were not enough to express how she felt right now.

He looked remorseful. 'I could be back in time for the birth. Ilias may recover.'

'He might. But I can't compete with a million people who need you. And that's how it should be. The needs of a million people outweigh my own. You have to go. I understand.'

'I want to stay.'

'But you *can't*!' Her voice broke. 'We knew this day would come. We were fools to think we could cheat it.'

'There must be a way?'

She nodded. 'There is. Accept your fate. It's always been there for you. Coming to England, meeting me...it could never stop that wheel from turning.'

He looked hurt. 'You know that I would stay if I could?'

She nodded, fresh tears running down her cheeks.

'You'll keep me informed?'

She frowned. 'How?'

'I'll leave my men. They can get messages to me.'

'No, Jamie. Take them all with you. Leave nothing behind.'

'I'm leaving *you* behind.'

She stared directly at him, through her tears and her pain. 'Exactly.'

He shook his head. 'I can't believe this is happening. Do we have to end this? Now?'

'We do. Because I can't live a half-life, Jamie. I've already done that for far too long…hiding from the world, living in the shadows. I've got to live for me now. For my children. And I deserve—*we* deserve—a happy, full life.'

'I can't walk away from my children.'

She winced. So he *could* walk away from her?

'But you will, Jamie. You've already made your choice. You've been called and you're going and you *should* go. Your brother is sick—has had a stroke. You need to see him, just in case his condition does not improve. You will be called upon to rule the country in his stead, and if he does not recover you will rule permanently. By going now you're choosing Majidar over us—as it should be. It's your duty.'

'You truly are the bravest woman I have ever known.'

She swallowed down her pain. 'You need to go now. Just *go*, Jamie.'

He looked away, his gaze taking in the twinkling Christmas tree, the wrapping paper discarded on the floor, the presents, the painting of his horse. And the small gift that she still had to open.

Jamie picked it up and held it in his hands. Staring at it for a moment, twisting it this way and that. Then he put it in his pocket, bent to pick up the teddy bears and gave her one last look.

'I love you, Freya MacFadden.'

She stared back, her heart breaking at this one last message, more tears falling freely down her face. 'And I love you, Jameel.'

And he went.

He turned his back and disappeared through the doorway.

Grief and pain tore sobs from her as she sank to her knees on the floor.

And on the television was the Queen, in her annual speech, talking to the nation. She focused on the Queen's face. A monarch addressing her people. Her whole life committed to her country.

How had she ever believed she could come between a man and such a love?

* * *

The house on Hayling Island had been closed up for a while.

Freya went through it, opening windows, letting in the aroma of the sea air despite the winter cold.

She turned up the thermostat on the central heating, made herself a mug of tea, and then stood outside on the small balcony and looked out to sea.

It was very still, calm, as if it was waiting for something. Grey-green, dully reflecting the grey sky above.

Down by the water she could see a dog walker, wrapped up in a thick jacket, throwing a tennis ball for three small dogs that chased after it happily.

This was what she needed—calm. The relaxed, unhurried way of life here, where no demands could be made of her and where she wouldn't have to find a brave face when inside she could feel herself crumbling.

She and Jamie had had their time cut short. Much too short. Both of them had believed—hoped—that they would have years…decades, perhaps. She'd begun to believe that her two sons would have a father. A great father. One who would adore them, teach them, raise them to be good boys. Good men.

Only now she would have that task alone.

What would she tell them about him? And when? As they got older they would begin to understand what a prince was, what a king was. Would they want to go to him?

She toyed with the idea of going with them one day. But she could only foresee agony in doing so. Meeting Jamie after many years... What if he had moved on? Married, as a king would be expected to do? What if he had a new family? Would she be welcomed in Majidar? Or spurned? Would Samuel and James always be known in Majidar as the King's illegitimate children?

And if they did visit there would always have to be another goodbye, and it wouldn't just be Freya who would be distraught afterwards it would be the boys, too, and *she* would be the one who would have to deal with the fallout. She would be the one to pick up the pieces of her children and slowly put them back together again.

Perhaps it might be best not to tell the boys who their father was? But the idea of lying to them, of manipulating the truth, made her feel sick.

What to do?

This was why she had come here to Hayling Island. To get some space. To think clearly. Not to see the nursery every day and be reminded of the ticking of the clock. She had mere weeks left of her pregnancy, and as if in reminder of that she felt her first Braxton Hicks contraction. A tightening of her belly. Her body preparing itself for the battle to come.

She rubbed her hand underneath her bump and breathed through it. There wasn't any pain, just a tightness, her belly going hard and rigid before slowly softening and relaxing again.

'I'll always be here for you,' she said to them, before going to close all the windows she'd opened. so she'd feel the benefit of the central heating.

She wanted to go down to the water, to walk along the beach and feel that sea air invigorate her lungs.

She grabbed her coat, hat and scarf and wrapped up well, then opened the door and stepped out, locking up behind her.

As she turned to begin her walk she felt something touch her cheek. Then her nose.

She looked up and saw that snow was finally beginning to fall, and it pained her to know that he was missing it.

'Oh, Jamie…'

Security guards lined the floor of the private hospital in which his brother the King lay. Escorted by Faiz and his own personal assistant,

Rafiq, Jamie strode down the corridor towards his brother's room.

He had been kept informed throughout his seven-hour flight back home on the Bakhari private jet. And the briefcase of documents awaiting his attention on the plane had reminded him of the life he had left behind when he'd first come to England.

He was trying his hardest to remain stoic, but his mind was a mess. He'd left her behind.

I left her behind!

Freya and his two babies. His sons. His heirs.

My heart.

But duty had called him and he felt helpless to try and fight it. He would never be the same again now that he'd been ripped in two.

Part of him hoped that when he walked into that hospital room and saw his brother lying in a hospital bed Ilias would open his mouth to speak and smile, maybe hold his brother in greeting, give him a hug, pat him on the back and say, *Welcome home, brother.*

That would be the best solution for them all.

His duty, his future, hung over him like a guillotine. He hated to refer to his noble duty in such a way, but it was how it had always felt to him. He'd never asked to be royal, never asked to be born into such a family, and being King had *never* interested him. Not once.

Leaving his country, his family, and flying thousands of miles away as a young man had taken a lot of courage, but he had followed his heart and done what he'd thought was right.

He came to his brother's room and placed his hand upon the door. The doctors had informed him that Ilias appeared to have a blood disorder. They weren't sure of it yet, but they were running tests.

He hoped they would learn what it was soon. So his brother could be treated and recover as quickly as possible.

He opened the door.

CHAPTER TEN

THERE WERE MONITORS sounding out the beats of his brother's heart.

He is alive.

But then he saw him—pale and wan against the hospital pillows, with his wife Jasmeen dutifully by his bedside, clutching his hand.

The shock of seeing him looking so ill stopped Jamie in his tracks.

'Jameel? You're here!' Jasmeen let go of her husband's hand and came over to embrace her brother-in-law.

'How is he?'

'The doctors say he is stable…but I have never seen him like this before.'

'Nor I.'

Jamie took a seat by his brother's bed and took hold of Ilias's hand.

'Ilias? It's Jameel. I'm here. I've come home.'

'He sleeps deeply since the stroke. It's like he has a tiredness that cannot be quenched.'

'Can he speak yet?'

'Sounds, but not words. It distresses him greatly. He tries to write, but he is right-handed, so it takes a while to read his words.'

Jamie squeezed his brother's fingers and felt tears sting the backs of his eyes. But he refused to cry here. Crying would be an admission of just how out of control he was, when he was desperately clinging to the one bit of hope that he still had.

'Ilias?'

His brother moaned and then began to blink, looking about him to find the source of his brother's voice.

'Nurgh...'

Tears appeared in Ilias's eyes when he saw his brother, and Jamie leant forward to kiss his brother's cheeks.

'I am here, brother. I am here.' He held his brother's face in his hands, touching his forehead to Ilias's.

His brother signalled for his writing pad and Jasmeen presented it to him.

I'm sorry you had to come home.

Jamie read the tight scrawl and smiled. 'Don't be sorry. You couldn't have known this was going to happen.'

You're about to become a father.

He nodded, thinking of Freya and her huge belly, of his hand resting on her abdomen, feeling the boys kick and stretch inside. He'd left them. Left them behind. Maybe never to see them again.

The ache in his chest was palpable. 'Yes.'

I did not want to do this to you.

'It's not your fault, brother. None of this is. I am just so grateful that you are still alive. You must fight hard, Ilias. Fight hard to get better.'

He turned to look at Jasmeen.

'Has he seen any physiotherapists yet?'

'They come three times a day.'

Ilias began to scribble again.

I don't think I can remain King like this.

Jamie's stomach dropped like a stone. 'You don't know what the future holds.'

Jasmeen gave a weak smile. 'The doctors hoped that his speech would be back by now, and though the weakness on his right side has yet to improve they hope with time that it will get a little better. But they are unsure of a full recovery.'

Jamie thought about what that meant for a moment. 'I see.'

'I have been talking to Ilias, Jameel. We have talked long and hard and taken everything into consideration. Ilias loves Majidar and its people so much—he believes it needs a strong leader. Right now he does not feel that that is him.'

Jamie shook his head and tried to implore his brother. 'It *is* you.'

'He wants to abdicate.'

Jasmeen's words dropped into the room like a grenade.

Abdicate? *Abdicate?* But if Ilias abdicated that would mean that he...

Jamie stood up and began to pace the room, coming to a stop by the window to stare out, far and wide over the desert in the distance, on the outskirts of the city. Freya was so far away.

'Nurgh...'

Jamie's eyes closed at the sound of his brother's voice. He felt awful. Pathetic. Thinking only of himself when his brother was in such distress and pain! What sort of man did that make him?

He turned to see that Ilias was holding up his writing pad. He read the words.

It doesn't have to be you.

It was New Year's Eve and the snow had been falling for a few days now. Thick, heavy flakes, tumbling silently, covering the world in a white blanket of softness.

It made everything look beautiful, but it had certainly put paid to Freya's ideas of getting some walks in. All the heavy rain there had been before the snow meant that there was a thick layer of ice beneath it, so the pavements and roads were treacherous.

The weather forecasters predicted more heavy snow and informed people that they should not travel unless they had to. Gritters were out, trying to line the roads, but they were fighting an endless battle.

Freya stayed in the small house, drinking lots of tea and eating plenty of warm, buttery toast in front of the log fire, flicking from channel to channel on the television to try and find something interesting to watch.

Today she'd found a few films and had settled in to watch those, aware that her Braxton Hicks contractions had been coming a lot more frequently just recently. This morning they had begun to start hurting, and every now and then she'd find herself having to stop and breathe, clutching onto the back of the sofa or a kitchen unit.

She dutifully called her mum and told her she was fine.

'I'm so worried about you, stuck out there with all this snow. What if you go into labour?'

'Then I'll call an ambulance, Mum. Stop worrying, I'm fine. I've got a few weeks left.'

'Two weeks left, Freya. *Two weeks*. Those babies could come any time.'

'Well, I *am* a midwife, Mum, so I'll know what to do.'

She managed to get her mum off the phone eventually, sighing heavily, and decided to run herself a bath.

A soak in warm water helped soothe her troubled nerves, and she was soon settled back on the couch with a nice cup of tea.

A sudden pain, low in her belly, had her gasping, and she had to reach under her bump to rub at her abdomen. Slowly the pain eased and she lay back again, wondering if she'd sat down awkwardly and maybe pulled a muscle?

But the pain was gone now, and she felt confident that she'd know if she was really in labour.

On the screen, a newsflash came up on the local news to say that most roads in the area were becoming inaccessible and it was recommended that people did not drive anywhere unless it was absolutely necessary.

She glanced out of the window. The snow was still falling and there were drifts right up to the ledge.

She'd never known it to snow like this before. Not down here. Not by the coast, where you'd imagine there'd be enough salt around to prevent it. But there it all was. A thick white blanket. Would it snow like this next year? Would she be able to let the twins out in it? See the wonder on their faces?

The thought made her smile—a smile that soon faded when she got another pain.

Oh, God. Is this it? Is this labour?

All her bravery, all her bravado because she was a midwife, went out of the window. She suddenly realised just how *alone* she was here, how isolated. And if she needed to call an ambulance would it be able to get here?

There was only a single road on and off the island, connected to the mainland by a bridge. What if that was blocked? Impassable?

She hauled herself up and began to breathe through the panic, pacing back and forth.

Okay...okay. This could just be early labour, and I'm a first-time mother so my labour could be hours yet. Plus, it could still die down. There's nothing to say that these pains will continue.

But they did. Every eight minutes she got a pain, and as the hours passed they increased to every five minutes.

She picked up the phone, but the line was

dead. She scrabbled in her handbag for her mobile and dialled 999.

'Ambulance, please.'

She was put through to Control and gave her address and situation. The guy on the phone told her that someone would be with her as quickly as they could, but because of the snowfall their ambulances were busy elsewhere. She was to try and find someone to be with her, so they could call again later if she needed to deliver at home.

Panicking, she put down her phone and began to think. Who could she get to help her? These properties were mostly summer holiday lets, and it was New Year's Eve!

A knock at the door had her struggling to walk over to it. Whoever it was, she would tell them what was happening. See if they could help her or if they knew someone else who could help. There were first responders on the island, surely? Perhaps they could get to her? She knew they didn't usually attend labouring women, but when needs must...

She grabbed hold of the door handle, turned the key and yanked the door open.

And there—shivering, wet, and very, very cold-looking—was Jamie. His face was red and glistening, his hair flattened by snowflakes.

Hesitantly, he smiled. 'I told you it would snow.'

'Jamie?'

'The one and only. Can I come in? Only I've been trudging through snow for the last couple of hours.'

'How did you know where to find me?'

But before he could answer another contraction ripped through her, and she gasped and let go of the door to bend over and put both hands on her knees to breathe through it.

'Freya? Are you in *labour*?'

She couldn't answer him for a moment. The contraction had completely obliterated her ability to talk whilst it was going on. The most she could do—the *only* thing she could do—was remain upright and breathe.

When it receded, and when normal thought and the real world returned, she stood straight again and looked at him with tears in her eyes. Her heart felt overwhelmed with relief and love for this man before her.

'For about four hours now.'

'*Four hours?* Why didn't you call for an ambulance? Stranded out here like this!'

'I did. They don't know when they can get to me. Apparently they're busy.'

He rummaged in his pocket for his mobile. 'I'll get someone here.'

He tapped at the screen and then held the

phone to his ear, shouting instructions in Arabic before snapping it shut again.

'I've got a paramedic being choppered in.'

'A helicopter? In this? How did you know where to find me?'

'There's a GPS tracker on your phone.'

'What?'

'They all have them. Don't worry—I didn't place some secret bug in it, or anything. I'm not that kind of guy.'

Another contraction began to build. 'Oh, God!'

She turned to lean against the stairs and felt Jamie's hands hold her steady and rub the small of her back. When it was done, he guided her back to the lounge so she could sit down.

'That last contraction was about a minute and they're coming fast.'

'You don't need to tell *me* that. I'm the one having them.'

'We need to prepare. Where are your towels? I'll put on some hot water, and we'll need scissors I can sterilise for cutting the cord—just in case.'

'Wait a minute. You can't come sweeping in here like a white knight. You need to tell me what's happening. How's your brother? Are you King?'

'Ilias has Von Willebrand's disease. He's being treated for it. The stroke has caused deficits, which hopefully will improve over time, but he has decided to abdicate, feeling that it's in the best interests of our country to have a ruler in full health.'

'He's *abdicated*? Can he do that?'

Her abdomen tightened with another vice-like contraction.

'Ohhhhh...'

She leaned forward and gripped the sofa, her eyes tightly shut as the feelings within her body overwhelmed her. Pain. Intensity. Breathing was the only thing she could manage for sure.

She felt Jamie take her hand and she gripped his fingers tightly, squeezing the blood from his digits. 'Oh, I think I need to push.'

'I'll need to check you first. Can I do that?'

She nodded quickly and removed her pyjama bottoms and underwear, wincing at the dying pain in her belly.

'I'll wash my hands. Do you have any gloves?'

Freya pointed into the kitchen. 'Beneath the kitchen sink are some latex gloves. Mum uses them for when she has to touch raw meat.' She tried to laugh, recalling her mother's squeamish nature.

'I'll be back in a moment.'

She lay back on the couch and wiped the sweat from her forehead.

Jamie was back. But how? If Ilias had abdicated, didn't that mean that Jamie was now

King? *Why* had he returned? Had they allowed him some kind of compassionate leave to be with her for when the babies arrived? So he could see them and *then* leave? She hoped not. Because even if that was good for him, it would be doubly difficult for *her*.

Having him here, holding her hand, mopping her brow, seeing the joy and love on his face as he looked at his sons and then having to wave him goodbye again… *No*. She couldn't allow that. She wouldn't survive it. The birth would be hard enough without being deserted right afterwards.

Jamie came back into the living room wearing a pair of latex gloves. 'Right, let's take a look. Has the contraction gone?'

'Yes. But maybe you should leave, Jamie?'

He looked up at her, confused. 'Leave? I just got here—and I don't think there's anyone more suitably qualified to help than me right now. I don't think I'll be fetching your elderly neighbour from next door, who needs a magnifying glass to read the evening paper.'

Now it was her turn to frown. 'Does he? How do you even *know* that?'

'I have *people*, remember? I'm going to examine you now. Try to relax.'

She lay back, opening her legs. 'Why does every man say that when he has to do an internal? Perhaps if men had a vagina they'd realise exactly how hard it is to *relax*!'

'Good point.' He smiled up at her. 'And good news. You're fully dilated. You can start to push with the next contraction.'

Freya's eyes finally began to leak tears of relief and happiness. 'I can?'

'You can.'

Jamie removed the gloves, pulling them inside out before discarding them in a small wastepaper bin. Then he pulled another pair from his pocket. 'Now—quickly—where are the towels kept?'

I can push. They'll be here soon. Samuel and James.

'Upstairs. Second door to the left is a small airing cupboard.'

'Don't do anything exciting without me.'

He kissed her on the cheek and raced upstairs and she watched him go, shocked by the feel of his kiss still upon her skin.

He seemed okay. He seemed as if he was in control. Was he really? Or was this all a front?

She still didn't know what was happening. Still didn't know whether he was staying. The hope that he might stay was building much too quickly, and she was struggling to fight it down, because she really wanted him to stay with her.

But reality told her that if Ilias had abdicated then Jamie was soon to be King, and he was only here on loan. His country had claimed him. And the knowledge of that was destroying her.

She began to cry.

Why was he doing this to her? Why had he come back and made her think there was hope? Made her think there was a chance for them still? It wasn't fair. Did he not know how hard it had been for her after he'd left the first time? If he did know then he wouldn't have done this.

She heard him come running back down the stairs and he appeared at her side with a huge pile of towels.

'You need to go.'

He frowned. 'Don't be ridiculous. I'm not going anywhere. What kind of man would I be to leave you in this state in the middle of a white-out?'

'A man with principles. I can't have you here, Jamie. Not like this! Not knowing you're going to leave me again!'

Another contraction hit and she heard nothing as his words faded beyond the pain she could feel surround her whole body. She sucked in a breath and, remembering all the advice she gave to labouring mothers, tucked her chin into her chest, curled around her baby and pushed down into her bottom.

It felt *good* to push! Excellent, in fact. There was almost relief there, because now she wasn't a passive observer of her pain, letting it roll over her in waves. Now she could do something about it!

She pushed against it, shoved back, using the pain of the contraction to start moving and birthing her babies.

'That's it, Freya! You're doing really well! Keep pushing right there. That's *it*!'

She let out a breath, then immediately sucked in another and began again. She managed two more huge breaths and two more pushes before the contraction died down and she could breathe properly again.

'Freya…' He took her hand and made her look him in the eyes. 'I'm not going to leave you. Not tonight. Not tomorrow. Not ever.'

Not ever?

'But—'

Another contraction began. *God, they're coming thick and fast now!* But she knew that was good. This was what was *meant* to happen.

'I can see a head, Freya! You're *doing* this! You're really doing this!'

When it was over, she reached down to touch the head of her first son and gasped when she felt it. 'Oh, my God!'

'With the next contraction his head will be born. Okay?'

She nodded, sucked in a breath, and began pushing again as the next contraction built.

'Keep pushing! Keep pushing! That's it—just like that. Now, stop! Pant it out!'

She panted, huffing away like an old-fashioned steam train, and then Jamie was telling her to give one last push.

She felt her son slither from her body and into Jamie's safe, waiting hands. He lifted Samuel up onto her belly. 'Here he is!'

'Oh, Jamie!' She grasped her son, her darling Samuel, ignoring all the stuff he was covered in—the white vernix, the smears of blood—and cried again out loud when her son opened up his lungs for the first time, letting out a long, strangled cry. 'Oh, he's so beautiful!'

He was. He was a good size—between six and seven pounds, she estimated—and with a thick, full head of dark hair like his father.

Jamie draped a couple of towels over his son, so he wouldn't get cold, then tied off the cord with string and cut it with the scissors he'd sterilised in a bowl of steaming hot water.

Then he looked at them. With *such* pride. 'I'm so proud of you.'

Freya beamed at him as she cradled her son. 'I can't believe he's here.'

'Safe and sound.'

'Thanks to you.'

'Thanks to *you*.'

She smiled and reached for him, so that he would lean forward and place a kiss upon her lips. A soft, gentle, reaffirming kiss. And then he stooped over his son's head and laid a kiss on his son's head, too.

'Oh, my! I can't believe this has happened so quickly!' She looked at him. 'And you're here! And you can *stay*?'

He nodded, smiling. 'I can stay.'

'How?'

'Ilias told me that I didn't have to take the throne. That my sister Zahra wants to do it. She's a good, strong woman. She's always wanted to get more involved with the running of things and she's a good choice. The people will look up to her.'

'But I thought you *had* to do it?'

'So did I. But what kind of King would I be? With my people knowing that I had deserted my own two sons to sit on the throne? Knowing that I had left behind the woman I loved? Above all, my people would want me to be happy—as my brother Ilias wanted me to be happy by letting me come to England in the first place. He knows my life is here now, as do my people. They will understand. And Zahra is much loved. She will make a fine monarch. A brilliant one.'

He could stay? For good? With her and Samuel and James and without any possibility of his desertion hanging over them?

Another contraction began to make itself known. 'It's starting again...'

'Do you want me to take Samuel?'

'Please. I don't want to squash him.'

She passed her firstborn safely over to Jamie and began to breathe through the contraction. Jamie would need to check her first, before she began pushing again. To make sure James was in a good position.

He checked her and smiled. 'He's head down. He's right there, Freya.'

'Okay. I can do this again, right?'

He smiled back at her. 'You can do *anything*!'

She had to believe him. Had to believe that she could give birth again even though she felt exhausted after delivering Samuel.

Hunkering down, she began to push.

It felt a little easier this time. She pushed and pushed, and before she knew what was happening the head was delivered.

'One more push and it will all be over.'

'I hope so!'

She gave a quick glance to Samuel, lying on the floor beside Jamie, wrapped up in towels, resting from the trauma of being pushed through the birth canal.

She'd often wondered if babies cried because

of the pain in their skull bones, overlapping to fit through, or whether it was just the shock of all the tiny alveoli in their lungs suddenly inflating for the first time. Maybe it was both?

But Samuel was here and he was safe, and he had a mother *and* a father, and of course she could do it again.

She sucked in a breath.

'That's it, Freya! Push! Harder!'

From somewhere she found a reserve she hadn't known she had. Whether it came from the knowledge that if she just did this one last push, as hard as she could, it would all be over, or whether she really did have that endless supply of energy distinctly found in women giving birth she didn't know. But she found it, and she used it, and she pushed with all of her might.

James was born. Into his father's hands and then up onto her stomach, the same as Samuel had been.

Crying with relief, she held him weakly, glad the pain was over, overjoyed that her babies were finally here, safe and well.

And Jamie…? Jamie was here to stay, it seemed. They could have the future that both of them wanted.

With the cord cut and the placentas delivered, Jamie sat himself next to her. They held a baby each. From above they could hear a helicopter, looking for a suitable place to land.

She smiled at her babies' little faces, gasping with delight at each tiny noise, each little snuffle, each beautiful yawn.

'Look at them, Jamie. They're so beautiful.'

'How could they not be with a mother like you?'

She smiled and leant her forehead against his. 'You're truly here to stay?'

'I'm here to stay. If you'll have me, of course.'

She turned to look at him. Looked deeply into those midnight-black eyes of his. Of course she wanted him! It was what she had always wanted but had been too afraid to admit, because she'd always thought he would have to desert her.

But that threat was gone now.

'Can I ask you something?'

She waited for him to look at her. He was still gazing at his sons with such love.

'Of course you can. You can ask me anything.'

'Will you marry me, Jamie?'

His gaze locked with hers and a delighted smile appeared upon his face. 'Yes. A thousand times, yes!' He leant forward until their lips touched.

Closing her eyes in exhausted delight, she kissed him back, pouring every ounce of her love for him into it. Oh, how she needed this man! She'd never known what was missing from her life. She'd convinced herself that her life was fine, hiding herself away on the night shift, pretending she was doing herself a favour.

That hadn't been any way to live. And Jamie had seen that. Known that. He'd looked beyond the mask she was wearing and called her on it. Not allowing her to get away with it.

He'd made her into the woman she'd been *before*. The woman she'd thought she would never be again.

'I love you, Jameel.'

He stroked her face. 'And I love *you*.'

EPILOGUE

MAJIDAR WAS MORE beautiful than she could ever have imagined. A vast desert kingdom, filled with a thriving populace that had roared and cheered their delight at Jamie's return for a two-week visit.

She'd been nervous. All those people! And she had taken Jamie from them. She had stopped him from being their king.

But the people were thrilled to have her there. They waved and smiled, and small children brought her bouquet after bouquet, which she passed back to the bodyguards who escorted them on their tour wherever they went. Everyone had treated her with deference, and she did not doubt their love for her as Jamie's wife.

Now, as she stood on the palace balcony, looking out across the oasis beyond, she felt Jamie's arms come around her from behind.

'How do you feel?'

She smiled and laid her head against his shoulder. 'Loved.'

'I told you they would all love you.'

She turned to face him, to look deeply into his eyes. 'But to be loved *this much*... I never would have thought it was possible.'

Jamie smiled back and lowered one of his hands to her slightly rounded abdomen. 'When should we tell them?'

She was pregnant again. This time carrying only one baby. She hoped it might be a girl, but she didn't really mind.

'Let's do it tomorrow. Let's tell the whole world.'

She knew it would be all right.

He smiled and pulled her towards him.

* * * * *

*If you enjoyed this story,
check out these other great reads from
Louisa Heaton*

*THEIR DOUBLE BABY GIFT
REUNITED BY THEIR PREGNANCY
SURPRISE
CHRISTMAS WITH THE SINGLE DAD
SEVEN NIGHTS WITH HER EX*

All available now!